Women Empowerment In New India

Compiled By

Dr. Hoori Nadir

Dr. Arshi Gouhar

Copyright

BUNDELKHAND PUBLICATION HOUSE

Registered Under MSME

ISBN Number : 978-81-985538-9-8

Book Type: Fiction

Book Formatting: BPH

Cover Designer - Dr. Hoori Nadir

Editor - Dr. Hoori Nadir

Printing- Amazon

Our Social Connection

Instagram: - bphbup

Twitter: - BundelkhandPub1

YouTube: - Bundelkhand Publication House

Email - bphbup@gmail.com

Disclaimer

This Book "**Women Empowerment In New India**" is based on Women Dealing with Domestic Violence in India. It is a tapestry woven with the threads of human experience. Within these pages, you will encounter narratives of survival, of strength forged in the fires of adversity, and of the unwavering hope that tomorrow holds the promise of a brighter future. We tried to analysis of this book free from errors. If you find any mistakes or error please tell us.

In case of any plagiarism found, the publisher will not be responsible for that. Writer/Poet will be solely responsible for his/her own content.

Acknowledgment

Writing this book on women empowerment has been a journey of reflection, learning, and deep appreciation for the countless individuals who have contributed to this cause. This work would not have been possible without the guidance, support, and encouragement of many people who believe in the power of change and equality.

First and foremost, I extend my heartfelt gratitude to the countless women whose courage and determination have paved the way for progress. Their stories, struggles, and triumphs have been a source of inspiration and motivation throughout this endeavor.

I am immensely grateful to my family and friends, whose unwavering belief in me and this project gave me the confidence to bring this book to life. Their encouragement and insightful conversations have enriched the perspectives shared within these pages.

To the mentors, educators, and advocates who have tirelessly worked towards gender equality—your dedication has shaped the foundation of this work. Your words, actions, and commitment to empowerment have left an indelible mark, and I hope this book serves as a tribute to your efforts.

A special thank you to the readers—those who seek knowledge, change, and empowerment. It is through understanding and collective effort that transformation takes place, and I am honored to have you embark on this journey with me.

Lastly, to every voice that has spoken up, to every hand that has lifted another, and to every heart that believes in a more equitable world—this book is for you.

With deep appreciation,

Dr Hoori Nadir Dr Arshi Gouhar

Preface

Empowerment is not merely a concept; it is a movement, a force that shapes societies, drives progress, and challenges deep-rooted norms. Women empowerment, in particular, has been at the heart of transformative change across centuries, breaking barriers, defying expectations, and forging new paths where none existed before.

This book is dedicated to the spirit of empowerment—not just as an idea but as a lived reality. It is an ode to the resilience, strength, and aspirations of women across the world, whose contributions have enriched families, communities, industries, and nations. It explores the significance of empowerment in various dimensions—economic, social, political, and personal—highlighting the struggles and triumphs that have marked the journey towards equality.

Women empowerment is not about comparison or competition; it is about creating a world where every individual, regardless of gender, has the freedom to realize their full potential. It is about dismantling stereotypes that have long confined women to predefined roles and expectations. It is about enabling education, ensuring economic independence, advocating for rights, and fostering environments where women can lead, innovate, and inspire.

Through the chapters that follow, we navigate the stories of women who have transformed adversities into opportunities, who have stood up against injustice, and who have become catalysts for change. We delve into historical struggles that paved the way for today's victories, examine contemporary challenges that demand urgent attention, and highlight the steps forward in the ongoing fight for gender equity.

This book is not merely a collection of narratives and reflections; it is a call to action. It urges us to rethink societal structures, to challenge norms that limit progress, and to champion inclusivity in every sphere of life. Women's empowerment is not a goal that belongs solely to women—it is a pursuit that benefits humanity as a whole. When women thrive, societies flourish, economies grow, and the future becomes brighter for generations to come.

As you turn the pages, may you find inspiration, courage, and insight. Whether you are a woman seeking motivation or an ally hoping to contribute to the movement, this book aims to fuel the conversation and reinforce the unwavering belief that empowerment is not a privilege—it is a right.

Let us embark on this journey together, towards a world where every voice is heard, every dream is valued, and every woman stands empowered.

Dr Hoori Nadir Dr Arshi Gouhar.

Compiler's Desk

Dr Hoori Nadir

The author is working as Assistant Professor in BBD University Lucknow. She authored so many books and written quality articles in reputed journals. She is internationally acclaimed writer and researcher. She is high headed great with establishing rapport with good interpersonal skillls.

The creation of safe workplace for Women POSH Initiative

Workplaces are not just about deadlines and meetings – they are sacred spaces where employees spend 8-10 hrs daily. Every employee brings their dreams, aspirations, and trust when they enter into an office mostly the fair gender called women. It should be strong consideration that they expect a safe, respectful, and nurturing environment in return. In India, POSH – the Prevention of Sexual Harassment Act – stands as a powerful commitment to this very idea.

What is POSH?

The POSH Act was passed in 2013, inspired by the Supreme Court's landmark Vishaka Guidelines laid down in 1997. It legally binds all workplaces, big or small, formal or informal, to take active steps against sexual harassment. More than just a law, POSH is a promise: that dignity and safety at work are non-negotiable.

Under POSH, companies must:

- Set up an Internal Complaints Committee (ICC).

- Conduct regular awareness programs for employees.

- Take complaints seriously, handle them sensitively, and resolve them fairly.

- Maintain confidentiality and protect the rights of both complainants and respondents.

The law is not only about punishing misconduct — it's about building a culture where such behaviour is not tolerated in the first place.

POSH and the Indian Work Culture

India's workplaces have come a long way. Once dominated by rigid hierarchies and silent acceptance, today's offices are striving to become spaces of openness and dialogue. POSH policies have played a crucial role in this evolution.

However, challenges remain. Many employees – especially in smaller towns or unorganized sectors – still hesitate to speak up. Some fear retaliation; others worry about being judged. In such cases, a policy document on paper is not enough. Real change happens when leaders lead by example, and organizations cultivate trust and empathy every day.

Why POSH Matters for Everyone

Sexual harassment doesn't just affect the person targeted. It poisons the whole work environment. It lowers morale, damages reputations, and breaks down teams.

When a company enforces POSH well, it sends out a clear message:

"We care about you. Your voice matters. Your safety matters."

And the impact is visible — higher employee satisfaction, better retention, stronger teamwork, and a workplace where people can truly focus on their growth.

Building a Future Beyond Compliance

Following the letter of the law is the first step. But truly progressive organizations go beyond compliance.

They foster inclusive policies, hold empathy-driven training, and create anonymous feedback channels. They recognize that safety and dignity are not just legal duties but moral ones.

Because, at the end of the day, a safe workplace is not built by rules alone. It's built by people – people who choose respect over indifference, support over silence, and fairness over fear.

Dr. Arshi Gouhar

Dr. Arshi Gouhar is an Author, Educationist,Counsellor and a Teacher Trainer. She is a resource person of CBSE and Master Trainer of Lead Group Academy .She has authored a series of computer books, her research papers are published in a number of National and International journals.She is an active participant in a number of anthologies also.

Breaking Barriers: Transforming India Through Women's Empowerment

Abstract: Women empowerment is the bedrock for the development and progress of a nation. In the Indian context, it is an ongoing process that in its various cycles has brought about radical changes in the society. This paper is a humble effort to explore the meaning, intent, significance, and the present state of the movement of women empowerment in India, highlighting the main challenges, the policy frameworks, progress, and also some important recommendations as well as learning for the future. The data highlights the gaps and successes in areas like political, social, economic and civil spheres while shedding light on overarching issues such as patriarchy, gender- based violence, glass ceilings, political issues and the social and economic disparities which create a colossal impediment towards realisation of true 'women empowerment'.

Keywords: Women empowerment, recommendations, patriarchy, gender-based violence, glass ceilings.

1. Introduction: Women empowerment is a qualitative term that stresses on holistic development of women in every sphere so that equity can be achieved to overcome the societal wrongs bestowed upon this gender. It relates to increasing the strength of women in social, economic, political, and legal platforms and also to ensure equal rights and opportunities for them in the country. With reference to Indian history, women empowerment has been an important issue because of the prevalent gender inequality since the later Vedic Period wherein the membership of women from the Samitis was annulled which begun the process of gender subordination. Although the Indian constitution guarantees equal rights and opportunities to women, Indian women are still a long ways away from getting their rightful place in the society.

2. **Historical Context**: India has witnessed a number of women's movements heralded by social reformers and common people alike. Women were accorded a high place in Indus valley civilisation and they had position of eminence even in Rig Vedic times wherein some hymns are attributed to women sages like Lopamudra, Apala etc. but this status

was shattered during the later vedic period and the denigration furthered in the medieval age. Some women reform movements happened during the bhakti and sangam age but they didn't have much effect on the general status of women in society it was only during the later medieval period that there was an upheaval in women empowerment movements taken up by the social reformers like Raja Ram Mohan Roy, Malabari, Ishwar Chandra Vidyasagar, Jyotirao Phule, Mahatma Gandhi, Ranade, Ambedkar etc all of which worked at eliminating social ills like sati, kulinism while advocating for women education, equality, widow remarriage and the like . Women reformers like Savitribai Phule, Annie Besant, Pandita Ramabai, Tarabai Shinde, Ramabai Ranade, Fatima Sheikh, Swarnakumari Devi, Sister

Nivedita, Kadambini Ganguly, Pandita Ramabai ,Sarojini Naidu, Kasturba Gandhi, Kamaladevi Chattopadhyay, Sucheta Kriplani, Aruna Asaf Ali, Devi Gaidenliu, Amrita Devi etc. contributed to the post-independence women's rights movement bringing about meaningful change in the society which is the reason behind their continued legacy.

The Indian Constitution firstly brought about equal voting rights for women, emphasized and grants equality (Articles 14, 15, and 16),brought about the concept of gender budgeting and the institutionalization of National Commission of women and NHRC, all of which are aimed at women emancipation however the patriarchal values have prevented the true transformation and progress in the field of Women Empowerment as enshrined in this living breathing document.

3. Present Status of Women in India: The present status of Indian women can be discussed under the following important heads.

3.1 Education: Talking about Female literacy,no doubt it has improved significantly, from 8.9% in 1951 to 70.3% in 2021. Government schemes like Beti Bachao Beti Padhao have further boosted school enrolment, but dropout rates among girls still remain high due to constraints like poverty, early marriage, lack of sanitation facilities in school and above all lack of awareness.

3.2 Employment: Indian women are moving forward in this front but there are glass ceilings existing that bind them to certain roles and limit the kind of positions they can hold.Several government schemes in India support female entrepreneurs by providing financial assistance, training, and mentorship. These include the Stand-Up India Scheme, Mudra Yojana, SHG's and the Udyogini Scheme, among others, which offer loans, subsidies, and training to help women start and grow their businesses. Some successful examples of women businesses in India are Lijjat Papad, Kudambshree and Metro.

Still women participation in the workforce remains low at around 20.3% (Periodic Labour Force Survey(PLFS, 2022). Informal employment and wage disparity continue to be the major concerns.

3.3 Health and Nutrition: Records shows that India has improved in maternal health indicators, with a decline in the maternal mortality rate.The government has taken some significant steps in this area like the Pradhan Mantri Matru Vandana Yojana (PMMVY). The basic objective of this project is to provide financial assistance to pregnant women and lactating mothers to encourage them to seek proper healthcare, maintain good nutrition, and practice early and exclusive breastfeeding. This financial support helps compensate for wage loss during pregnancy and postpartum, enabling mothers to take adequate rest and focus on their health and the newborn's well-being.

However, access to reproductive healthcare, menstrual hygiene, and nutrition for women still needs urgent attention, especially in rural areas and for this a revamp of Anganwadi centres and primary health centres is needed. Besides, a shift towards preventive care is needed.

3.4 Political Participation: Indian women were seen before Independence also on the political front participating actively in all the movements in the struggle for independence. Women's political representation has improved through reservations in Panchayati Raj Institutions (33%), but in Parliament, women constitute only around 15% of Lok Sabha members. The Women's Reservation Bill (2023)legislation aims to reserve 33% of seats in the Lok Sabha and state assemblies for women, including those reserved for Scheduled Castes and Scheduled Tribes.

Yet, true power hasn't penetrated in female hands since practices like Sarpanchpati exist that subordinate even the women in power.

4. Key Challenges

4.1 Patriarchy and Gender Norms: Patriarchy represents a culturally endorsed set of norms, beliefs, and practices entrenched within societal systems, perpetuating gender inequality between men and women. The concept of patriarchy has traditionally been used to analyse women's oppression, subordination, and subjection in a social order where men are perceived as superior to women. Deep-rooted patriarchal beliefs restrict women's mobility, decision-making, and freedom. Practices like child marriage, dowry, and honour killings are still prevalent in some areas.

4.2 Gender-Based Violence: India has one of the highest rates of gender-based violence, including domestic violence, sexual assault, and workplace harassment. Legal recourse exists like Protection of Women from Domestic Violence Act, 2005, The Dowry Prohibition Act, 1961, but enforcement and victim support are often lacking. In this aspect Sambal Scheme, One stop centres etc have been introduced to address the lacunae.

4.3 Economic Inequality: India was ranked 127 out of 146 countries in the Global Gender Gap Report, 2023, and faces the perennial issue of "missing women" from the workforce. Lack of asset ownership, financial literacy, and access to formal employment restrict economic empowerment. Women are overrepresented in low-paying and unpaid labour sectors.

5. Government Initiatives and Policies: A number of initiatives have been taken by Indian government to attain women empowerment. Some of them are mentioned below:

Beti Bachao Beti Padhao - aims at eliminating female foeticide and promoting girl child education.

Mahila Shakti Kendra - provides support and services for women in rural areas.

Pradhan Mantri Ujjwala Yojana - improves women's health by providing LPG connections.

National Policy for Women (Draft 2016) - focuses on economic empowerment, education, and safety.

Key Laws and Policies: The important acts and laws made in this area are:

The Dowry Prohibition Act, 1961: Prohibits the giving and taking of dowry.

The Protection of Women from Domestic Violence Act, 2005: Provides legal remedies for victims of domestic violence.

The Sexual Harassment of Women at Workplace (Prevention, Prohibition and Redressal) Act, 2013 (PoSH Act): Addresses and prevents sexual harassment in workplaces.

The Equal Remuneration Act, 1976: Guarantees equal pay for equal work

The Maternity Benefit Act, 1961: Ensures maternity leave and protection for pregnant women.

The Prohibition of Child Marriage Act, 2006: Sets the legal age for marriage at 18 for girls.

The Immoral Traffic (Prevention) Act, 1956: Addresses human trafficking, particularly of women and girls.

The Medical Termination of Pregnancy Act, 1971: Regulates termination of pregnancy.

The Special Marriage Act, 1954: Facilitates marriages regardless of caste or religion.

The Indecent Representation of Women (Prohibition) Act, 1986: Prohibits portrayal of women in an indecent or derogatory manner.

National Policy for Women (2001): Aims to eliminate discrimination and promote the advancement and development of women.

6. Constitutional Provisions: The Indian Constitution guarantees several rights for all women, including equality before the law, prohibition of discrimination based on sex, and equal opportunities in employment. It also allows for positive discrimination in favour of women to address historical disadvantages. These rights are as follows:

Article 14: Right to Equality: Guarantees equal rights for all citizens, including women.

Article 15: Prohibition of Discrimination and Special Provisions: Prohibits discrimination based on sex and allows for special provisions in favour of women.

Article 16: Equality of Opportunity: Ensures equal opportunities in employment.

Article 39: Directive Principles of State Policy: Includes provisions for equal pay for equal work and legal aid.

Article 42: Just and Humane Conditions of Work and Maternity Relief: Provides for maternity relief and just conditions of work.

Articles 243-D(3), 243-D(4), 243-T(3), and 243-T(4): Reservation in Local Bodies: Guarantees women's participation in local government.

7. Change in Mindset of Society and Media

Women Empowerment is all about mindset and perspective. To ensure proper women empowerment, we have to change our mindset as a society. NGOs, self-help groups (SHGs), and women's collectives have played a critical role in grassroots empowerment. Media and digital platforms have helped amplify women's voices but still there is a long way to go in order to achieve the required Women Empowerment.

8. Further Implications

In order to attain proper women empowerment, we as a country have to aim progress in the following areas:

Education: We have to ensure universal access to quality education without the distinction of sex.

Skill and Vocational Development: We have to ensure result oriented vocational trainingspecially designed for women

Economic Inclusion: We have to promote entrepreneurship, digital literacy, and asset ownership amongst the women.

Legal Reforms: Strengthening the law enforcement, legal aid, and judicial processes for gender-based crimes can contribute in this area.

Awareness: Gender sensitization and challenging patriarchal norms through awareness campaigns can be of great help.

Incorporating Technology: Leveraging digital tools for women's safety, learning, and financial inclusion is much required.

9. Conclusion

The Women empowerment in India needs a dedicated push to witness a cycle of continuous improvement. The status of women needs an overhaul if we want to bring about meaningful change in the society. Existing mechanisms need checks and support while on ground workers need handholding. Scope of Women empowerment needs broadening from mere equality and justice to inclusion of dimensions of STEM and gloablisation to herald in economic development coupled with sustained progress. The dream of a gender-equal India should be treated as a common goal and can only be achieved through collaboration and coordination.

As quoted by our first Prime minister, Mr. Jawaharlal Nehru, "To awaken the people, it is the women who must be awakened. Once she is on the move, the family moves, the village moves, the nation moves."

Dr. APJ Abdul Kalam in his first speech as President in Central Hall of Parliament, July 25, 2002 quoted, "When the women are empowered, society with stability gets assured"

Shulamith Firestone, a key figure in radical feminism, argued that women's liberation requires a fundamental shift in society, particularly through the elimination of the biological basis of oppression

References:

Ministry of Women and Child Development. (n.d.). Government of India initiatives. https://wcd.nic.in

National Family Health Survey (NFHS-5). (2021). India fact sheet 2019-21. International Institute for Population

Sciences (IIPS) and Ministry of Health and Family Welfare. http://rchiips.org/nfhs/NFHS-5_FCTS/India.pdf

National Statistical Office. (2022). Periodic Labour Force Survey (PLFS), Annual Report 2021-22. Ministry of Statistics and Programme Implementation, Government of India. https://mospi.gov.in

Office of the Registrar General & Census Commissioner, India. (2011). Census of India 2011. https://censusindia.gov.in

UN Women India. (2021). Women's empowerment in India: Key issues and policy recommendations. https://india.unwomen.org

Index

1. **Adarsh Kumar Varshney**

2. अनुज पटैरिया आदिशेष

3. **AINA RAFAT**

4. **Manjeet Kaur**

5. **SONU RAJAK**

6. **Sarita Mahiwal**

7. **Nilofar Farooqui Tauseef**

8. **Rohit Jain**

9. **Tanveer Sarvar**

10. **Dr. Swati Srivastava**

11. डॉ शरीफ़ ख़ान

12. **Rahul Raikwar**

13. **Dr Parul Yadav**

14. डॉ नीलू समीर

Adarsh Kumar Varshney

Adarsh Kumar Varshney is from Gwalior (M.P.) He likes to study books, listen music and observe small things. He has keen interest in writing. His achievements are yet to come to him. He is pursuing MBBS and want to serve the nation and last but not the least, spread happiness the most he can.. "Medical student by day, wordsmith by night. Pursuing MBBS and exploring the world of literature through anthologies. Passionate about observing life's nuances and spreading joy through simple, genuine interactions."

जवाब देना आता है...

लड़ जायेंगी ये

भिड़ जायेंगी ये।

कुछ भी करो

अपनी ज़िद पर अड़ जायेंगी ये।

और अगर अकड़ दिखाई

तो अकड़ में तुमसे और बढ़ जायेंगी ये।

बदतमीज़ को जवाब देना

जिसको सबसे अच्छा आता है,

हर बात को सही ढंग से बताना

जिनको भाता है,

तब भी न जाने क्यों

ये पुरुष अपनी पौरुषता

का क्यों ज्ञान बखाता है।

प्यार और कोमल का उलट रूप

जिनके अंदर बस्ता है,

किसी को लपेट लिया

तो उसकी हालत खस्ता है।

बेवजह उलझने से अच्छा

नाप लो अपना रास्ता है,

गायत्री से कब दुर्गा बन जाए

उसके लिए जो समझे इनको सस्ता है।

आवाज़ जो दब गयी...

वो जो दब गयी अब भला कैसे उठेगी?

इतना सहने के बाद वो कैसे बोल सकेगी?

आईने के सामने खुद से कैसे नज़र मिला सकेगी?

अपनी विपदा कैसे किसी को बात सकेगी?

समझदार है इतनी कि किसी को कुछ न बताती,

पर क्या और कब तक वो खुद को समझाती।

उम्मीद के परे अपना जज़्बा दिखाती,

हर अत्याचार के बाद अपनी बात कैसे दिखलाती।

आवाज़ उठने पर जो हर जिल्लत झेल लेती है,

हर ज़िद अपने परिवार की वो खुशी खुशी पूरी कर देती है।

फ़िर भी प्यार से बात कर लेने पर,

हर बात को प्यार से खेल लेती है।

जितना भी कष्ट हो प्यार से

सब कुछ सह लेती है।

अनुज पटैरिया आदिशेष

ये लेखक है श्री अनुज पटैरिया आदिशेष जी ।इनकी शिक्षा परा स्नातक रसायन विज्ञान से पूर्ण हुई है ।ये उत्तर प्रदेश के बेसिक शिक्षा विभाग में प्रधानाध्यापक पद पर कार्यरत हैं। इन्होंने लगभग 200 कविताओं का सफल लेखन किया है । इन्हे विद्या भूषण पुरस्कार, मुंशी प्रेमचंद साहित्य अकादमी पुरस्कार, हृदय कमल साहित्य सम्मान जैसे लगभग 30 पुरुस्कार प्राप्त हुए है ।मैं इनके कुशल और अलौकिक भविष्य की कामना करता हूं।

छलकर उसका अंतर्मन

नारी नारी नारी नारी

नारी नारी करते रहते ,

छलकर उसका अंतर्मन ,

नीचता अपनी सींचते रहते ।

क्या नारी इतनी कमजोर है ,

कि उसको जरूरत तुम्हारी है ,

जिसकी गोद में सृजन प्रलय पले,

नही गुलाम वो तुम्हारी है ।

नारी से मकान घर बने ,

देवताओं सा स्वर्ग ।

कलुषित मानसिकता से ,

करो ना उसका बेड़ा गर्ग ।

नारी कुछ नहीं सब कुछ है ,

ममता त्याग की मूरत है ।

नारी हर घर की एक

अनकही सी जरूरत है ।

AINA RAFAT

Aina Rafat is an assistant professor at the School of Management, BBD University, with over five years of experience in teaching business administration. Her expertise spans Green Marketing, Digital Marketing, Microfinance, Rural Management, Behavioural Science, Ethics, and Value Education. A dedicated researcher, she has published papers in ABDC and ESCI -listed journals, presented papers at various national and international conferences and contributed chapters to edited books. She is known for her organized, detail-oriented approach and commitment to continuous learning.

Women empowerment: A lie told loud enough to sound like truth

Aurton ne janam diya mardon ko,
Mardon ne usee bazar diya

Jab chaha masla kuchla, jab chaha
dhutkar diya!

-Sahir Ludhianvi

And yet! We dare to talk about WOMEN EMPOWERMENT, a phrase that's beautiful, polished, and marketable but feels like a charity, a grand favour.

What empowerment?

The one where we praise women in speeches and silence them in decisions?

The one where we put her on posters, but never in positions of power?

The one where we still measure her character by the length of her clothes and obedience in her voice?

Let's be honest!

Our society does not want empowered women.

It wants well-behaved and well-tamed women.

Pretty-looking Barbie dolls, who dream less, speak less and never forget their limits.

Women empowerment is a hollow Instagram-filtered scam, a sick joke and a nicely packaged lie, a marketing gimmick that is sold at social media, conferences and universities, while behind closed doors women are still paraded as trophies, and have the same chains around their necks just, painted gold to make them look prettier.

We tell our women-

- To be bold but not too bold.
- To work but not to forget household chores.
- To be successful but not to forget their duties.
- To be free but to stay within their boundaries.

Every forward-taking step of women is met with a gate, a glass ceiling, a character assassination and backhanded slaps disguised as a concern or cultural boundary.

We do handpick a few women and exhibit them as proof that "the system works", while millions of women are told to shrink, apologise, sacrifice, compromise and stay silent because we as a world are not ready for their full power.

We celebrate women on social media and punish them for wanting respect, equality and fairness in marriage, offices and streets.

It's high time we should stop pretending!

The reality is society fears women's strength. It fears what will happen when women stop asking for permission and start acknowledging their worth.

Real empowerment isn't about giving women a seat at the table but letting them burn the table and rebuild it on their own terms.

The real question is not about empowerment, the real question is:

- How long do we keep selling this illusion to our women?

- How long do we keep feeding women crumbs and calling it a feast?

- How long do we keep policing their dreams while pretending to celebrate them?

If we truly want our women to feel empowered then it's time to stop talking and start dismantling the system, stop saying and start practising it, stop marketing and start meaning it. Women empowerment is not a festival; it is a fight, and if you are not ready to fight for it, then stop pretending that you believe in it.

Manjeet Kaur

Manjeet kaur is an Assistant Professor in the Department of Management at Babu Banarsi Das University, Lucknow. She is a Ph.D research Scholar in Amity Business School, Amity University, Lucknow. She has been in academics for the past 10 years and in corporate in Human Resource Department. Her areas of expertise is Human Resource Management, Industrial Relations,Stress Management, Employee Wellbeing, and SPSS. She has presented various research papers and attended various International and National conferences.

Women Empowerment

Amidst the increasing crime against women in the same world....

Dear Women....Please remember

You have known that it is the people who have ruined how you feel about them.

Irrespective of Mars or Venus, it is the people who will one moment, make you feel how important you are to them and how meaningless your existence is at other times.

My dear Pretty Women...It is the people who make you feel on top of the world one moment, and in the other moment, you are invisible to them.

It is the same people who were once overwhelmed with your care, happiness, and they are the ones who can empty you like an ancient dry well.

It is the people who destroy how you think about them, once you trusted them, loved them, and how they belittled you, betrayed you, and shattered you at the end

Oh my dear, dear woman, you have always known that it is the same people whom you have talked heart out for hours, days and night and yet they are the ones who made you go silent with your words.

Oh my dear lovely ladies, these people who tell you that you are everything to them and they can't live without you it is the same people who don't even think twice before they can cut your souls apart with their words,with their actions...they have left scars that will never fade ..

My little girl, these people who think that you are weak, incapable, and insufficient of yourself they don't know that whatever they did, eventually they made you brighter, stronger, and braver.

So, before you doubt your own existence.. just remember you are the light, you are the wisdom, you are the love... and you are capable of everything.

You are yourself a miracle, you bring magic to this world... do not ever let your light diminish because of them.

They do not know your hassles, what you have been through, what you came through, your silent struggles.. So my strong strong lady, you need to brush that cute little hair of yours up your forehead..

keep your head held high and walk like a Queen..

Remember, please just remember, yes people disrupt things they just break you, make you question your worth ..They play with your emotions..your innocence...

Oh my pretty Girl, these people whom you believe to understand you, who promised to keep you untouched by the worldly things, they crush all of that and then they say..

Oh girl, you have changed, you're not the same anymore...

Please remember in those moments of darkness, to what you already know.

You need to heal, you need to inhale fresh air...

You wanted to be as innocent as a baby, you wanted to be faithful. you wanted to be loyal You wanted to be love, trust and. You wanted to be forgiving..

Dear Women,..Just so you know that you are out of this world.

You wanted to catch some moments of love and passion....

You wanted to catch those feelings of happiness and peace....

You wanted to breathe in that wavy, cold breeze..

You wanted to go with the flow....

You wanted to be you...

You wanted to be free....

Just so you remember what you already know...

You are capable of doing whatever you want to do...you are beautiful, you are intelligent..

And just so you don't forget you are awesome...

SONU RAJAK

SONU RAJAK (Assistant Professor) MANUU College of Teacher Education Darbhanga (Bihar), India. A Central University Ministry of Education Government of India. Mr. Sonu Rajak serves as an Assistant Professor in Maulana Azad National Urdu University (MANUU) posted at College of Teacher Education in Darbhanga, Bihar. He holds a Master of Arts (M.A.) in History, Master of Education (M.Ed.), and has qualified the University Grants Commission National Eligibility Test (UGC NET) in Education.

Women's Empowerment in India: Policy, Progress and Challenges

Abstract

Empowerment of women in India is an ontological development and socio cultural concern, determined by state policy dynamics, patriarchal discourse, and structural inequalities. The article critically examines flagship government initiatives like Beti Bachao Beti Padhao, Ujjwala Yojana, and PM Jan Dhan Yojana and their contribution to social, economic, and political empowerment of women.Drawing on feminist theoretical perspectives (liberal, radical, intersectional) and empowerment theory, the research draws on secondary data and content analysis of national opinion polls and policy records to measure progress and ongoing gaps. Tremendous progress has been achieved in domains such as education, maternal health, financial inclusion, and popular political participation, but fundamental barriers such as pay gaps, digital exclusion, care work, and underrepresentation in higher order politics continue to hold back effective empowerment. It is concluded in the article that narrowing this gap between policy and practice can be achieved through structural reform, better implementation, legal literacy, and intersectional and community-based interventions to lead to inclusive and transformative results.

Keywords: Women's Empowerment, Gender Equality, Feminist Theory, Policy Implementation, Social Justice, Intersectionality

Introduction

Women empowerment has become one of the key themes in global development discourse, especially during the 21st century. In the Indian context, where there is a complicated interplay between traditional norms, patriarchal values, and socio economic inequalities, women empowerment not only remains a developmental issue but also a social change imperative. It entails granting women access to resources, decision making power, involvement in governance, and the ability to acquire education, employment, and health care (Kabeer, 1999; Malhotra, Schuler & Boender, 2002). Empowerment is, thus, both a process and outcome where women are able to exercise agency, voice, and the power to challenge and transform the power relations that act as their stumbling blocks (Cornwall & Edwards, 2010). In the past few decades, India has sought to actively close the gender gap and uplift the status of women through constitutional safeguards, policy measures, and targeted programs. Welfare schemes for women like Beti Bachao Beti Padhao, Stand Up India, Ujjwala Yojana, and legal amendments in acts including the Prohibition of Child Marriage Act, 2006, and Protection of Women from Domestic Violence Act, 2005, speak to the inherent will of the state machinery to guarantee the welfare of the women.Today, as literacy rates for women in India continue to rise, their employability has also improved. At the grassroots level, we've seen significant political empowerment thanks to a 33% reservation in Panchayati Raj Institutions (PRIs) set by the Ministry of Women and Child Development in 2023. However, despite this remarkable progress, the reality on the ground reveals a stark contrast. Despite advancements, women continue to confront serious challenges such as gender-based violence, limited access to quality education and healthcare, disparities in wages, and underrepresentation in leadership positions (UNDP, 2022). The World Economic Forum's Global Gender Gap Report (2024) places India at 127th out of 146 countries, underscoring persistent structural obstacles that prevent women from achieving true equality and empowerment. Under these contradictions in which state policy initiatives coexist with inherent socio cultural inequalities there is a necessity for examining women's empowerment using strong theoretical frameworks. Theoretical frameworks assist us to decipher the systemic dynamics of gender oppression, the function of institutions, and the power dynamics and agency. Feminist theories, particularly liberal feminism, radical feminism, and intersectional feminism, provide valuable insights into how legal rights, social roles, and identities intersect to affect the empowerment process (Tong, 2009; Crenshaw, 1989).Empowerment theory, introduced by Rappaport in 1981 and later expanded upon by Zimmerman in 1995, offers a psychosocial lens through which we can understand how individuals and communities gain control over their lives.This study's theoretical framework is essential because it is consistent with important feminist and empowerment theories for analyzing policies critically, gauging actual progress, and illuminating persistent issues. By moving beyond superficial metrics and indicators, this method contributes to the development of a more comprehensive, context-specific understanding of women's empowerment in India.

This study aims to examine the current status of women's empowerment in India, focusing on the effectiveness of government policies, the noticeable advancements in recent years, and the enduring challenges that still impede inclusive development. Our research objectives include analyzing various policy frameworks such as Beti Bachao Beti Padhao, Ujjwala Yojana, and legal reforms to see how theyve contributed to women's social, economic, and political empowerment. We also want to determine whether these initiatives have really tackled the multifaceted issues faced by women in India. In addition, the study aims to identify the gaps between policy creation and on the ground execution, while exploring how feminist theories can help us better understand the structural and cultural dimensions of empowerment. The literature currently in publication shows that women's empowerment in India has received extensive discussion across academic and policy and developmental forums. Kabeer (1999) and Malhotra et al. (2002) argue that empowerment requires more than resource access because it means exercising agency to achieve meaningful results. Sen (1999) and Nussbaum (2000) build upon this concept by presenting the capabilities approach which states that authentic empowerment emerges from the ability to make choices and take control of opportunities. To analyze these issues, this research adopts a qualitative research strategy based on secondary data analysis. It is dependent on government reports, national surveys, academic writing, NGO reports, and international databases in seeking relevant data. Content analysis is adopted to research policy reports, comparing intended outcomes to real outcomes. Feminist theoretical constructs liberal feminism, radical feminism, and empowerment theory guide understanding of the ideological foundations of empowerment in India. Crenshaw's (1989) intersectional theory is applicable to women's studies, as it outlines how caste, class, and religion intersect and affect women's lives in multicultural India. NFHS 5 (2021), Ministry of Women and Child Development (2023), and United Nations Development Programme (2022) also assert that India is faced with gender violence, wage inequality dialectics, and low female labor force participation as political participation and literacy rise. Despite progressive policies, patriarchal resistance and inadequate policy implementation reaching the rural and marginal sections to an extent very high empowerment becomes unbalanced, according to literature.

Content

Policies for Women Empowerment in India:

During the past decades, the Indian Government has initiated a series of policies and legislative measures to empower the socio-economic and political position of women. The policies encompass concerns ranging from education, health, economic empowerment, legal protection, and digital inclusion. At the national level, the Beti Bachao Beti Padhao (BBBP) scheme initiated in 2015 was aimed at improving the declining child sex ratio and survival, protection, and education of the girl child. Nevertheless, according to reports tabled by the Comptroller and Auditor General (CAG, 2018), over 60% of the amount under BBBP was spent on advertisement via the media, and hardly any on-ground activity.

Within health and household welfare, the Pradhan Mantri Ujjwala Yojana (PMUY) launched in 2016, granted free LPG connections to over 9 crore poor women in order to reduce indoor air pollution and health hazards from traditional chulhas. Women were empowered through the scheme by ending their reliance on biomass and freeing them from unpaid working hours (MoPNG, 2022). Similarly, schemes such as the Janani Suraksha Yojana and Mission Indradhanush were launched to improve the health of mothers and children. Economically, Stand-Up India and MUDRA Yojana have attempted to promote entrepreneurship by lending and supporting small women-owned businesses. The National Policy for Skill Development and Entrepreneurship (2015) also includes gender sensitization as the key strategy to build skills and employability of women. Further, state-specific schemes such as Kanyashree (West Bengal) and Ladli Lakshmi Yojana (Madhya Pradesh) provide direct financial assistance to incentivize girls' education and delay early marriage. Despite their positive intent, most of these policies suffer from challenges related to underfunding, fragmented implementation, and lack of awareness among beneficiaries (NITI Aayog, 2020).

Progress Made in Women Empowerment:

India has seen measurable gains on various aspects of women empowerment over the last two decades, mainly in education, health, access to finance, and local-level political participation. Women's literacy has risen to approximately 71.5%, as per NFHS 5 (2021), from 65.5% in NFHS

4. This suggests an increase in access to education. One of the most impressive successes has been women's political participation at the village level. The 73rd and 74th Constitutional Amendments in 1992 provided 33% reservation for women in Panchayati Raj Institutions, resulting in the election of more than 1.3 million women representatives (Ministry of Panchayati Raj, 2022).There is proof that women-headed local governments tend to concentrate on water, sanitation, and health matters, therefore resulting in more effective governance results (Chattopadhyay & Duflo, 2004). So, here's the thing maternal care in India? It's actually come a long way. I mean, the numbers don't lie: the maternal mortality rate dropped to 97 per 100,000 live births in 2022. Back in 2014-16, it was sitting at 130. That's a big jump, or, well, drop.

Whatever. You get it. Most of that's 'cause the government finally got its act together more hospital births, better check ups for moms, that whole deal. Now, let's talk money because, honestly, everything comes down to it. The PMJDY thing? Game changer. Over 23 crore women opened bank accounts. That's wild. Once you've got your own account, and you're hooked into all those direct benefit transfers, you don't have to wait around for someone else to hand you cash. It's your money, your rules. Major upgrade in freedom, if you ask me.

Challenges to Women Empowerment in India

Women are confronted with structural constraints like wage discrimination, occupation segregation, work place safety concerns, and coercion to accept home work. Even the educated women tend to exit jobs because of the weight of unpaid domestic work that is roughly three times more for women compared to men (OECD, 2021). Another significant hurdle is the digital divide. Digital infrastructure has increased, but mobile internet access is available to only around 33% of rural Indian women (GSMA, 2022). This restricts them from utilizing e-governance, online learning, and digital business opportunities. Patriarchal thinking and cultural norms are still constraining women's agency, especially in rural areas and conservative environmentsEarly marriage, mobility restrictions, son preference, and a lack of support from family limit many girls and women from achieving their potential. Additionally, legal consciousness and access to redress are low. Legal procedures and right awareness are conceived as impossible hurdles beyond reach for the majority of women. One-Stop Centres for aggrieved women are inadequately accessed because of poor outreach and delay in procedures. Lastly, women's presence in higher political seats is still lacking. In spite of considerable grassroots-level presence, women hold less than 15% Lok Sabha members (Parliament of India, 2024). The billowing over two decades in the pending state of the Women's Reservation Bill, providing 33% reservation within Parliament and state legislatures, reflects political reluctance toward gender equality in the political sphere. . marriage, mobility restrictions, son preference, and lack of family support constrain a great many girls and women from realizing their potential. Also, legal awareness and access to redressal mechanisms are low. Legal processes are perceived as inaccessible and intimidating by most women, who also do not know their rights.. Initiatives such as One Stop Centres for women in crisis are inadequately accessed because of inadequate outreach and procrastination by the bureaucracy.Finally, women holding higher political positions are still inadequate. Despite huge grassroots level presence, women have less than 15% members of Lok Sabha (Parliament of India, 2024). The over two decade long pending condition of the Women's Reservation Bill, which provides for 33% reservation in Parliament as well as state legislatures, reflects political resistance towards gender equality in politics.

Discussion and Conclusion

The women's empowerment in India portrays a multifaceted and sometimes contradictory picture. On the one hand, we have readily apparent advances in education, financial inclusion, maternal health, and grassroots political representation. Programs instituted by the government like Beti Bachao Beti Padhao, Ujjwala Yojana, Stand-Up India, and PMJDY have incontestably helped in raising the millions of women through the provision of resources and access to fundamental rights and opportunities. Constitutional changes that facilitate women's political involvement at the panchayat level have contributed considerably to changing the priorities of governance at the grassroots level. Yet this advance is uneven, and often not deeply ingrained. Patriarchy, socio-cultural inhibitions, violence against women, unpaid care work, and weak legal awareness still seriously impede the empowerment process. The glaring difference between policy intention and real implementation comes to the fore when programmes such as BBBP have been criticized for being performative (expenditure in great part on mass media advertisements) rather than effective on the ground. Likewise, programmes providing financial or material support tend not to tackle deeper social norms and institutional inequalities. One of the central conclusions of this research is the ongoing disconnect between the formulation of policies and their effective implementation. Inadequate inter-departmental coordination, lack of outreach, under-financing, and poor monitoring mechanisms weaken the overall effectiveness of even the best intentioned programs. In addition, although there has been significant advances in women's participation in local government, their being under-represented at the national and state legislative levels reflect a reluctance to transfer actual political power to them. The long awaited Women's Reservation Bill is an example of such hesitation. The application of feminist theory traditions liberal, radical, intersectional feminism, and empowerment theory has established that empowerment is not only about opportunities but also about confronting the more fundamental issues of power, agency, and identity. As Crenshaw's theory of intersectionality brings home, empowerment needs to take into account how gender interacts with caste, class, religion, and rural-urban divisions to produce distinctive axes of disadvantage. A rural village Dalit woman has much more in her way than a middle-class urban woman under the same policy framework.

Overall, women's empowerment in

India remains a work in progress, with great accomplishments but deep-seated issues as well. It cannot be quantified solely by surface criteria such as literacy or bank account openings. actual empowerment will demand a change in the structure altering social norms, enhancing implementation instruments, enhancing legal understanding, and guaranteeing inclusive participation in decision-making at all levels. Bottom-up strategies, ongoing monitoring and assessment, and community centered interventions must take priority for policy to become actual change. Then and only then can India draw nearer to fulfilling its dream of a just, equitable, and gender equal society.

Indian women's empowerment reflects a seemingly intricate and occasionally contradictory scene according to the evidence. There has been evident progress in certain areas, such as education, maternal health, financial inclusion, and political representation at the local level (NFHS 5, 2021; Ministry of Panchayati Raj, 2022). Government initiatives like Beti Bachao Beti Padhao (BBBP), Pradhan Mantri Ujjwala Yojana (PMUY), Stand Up India, and Pradhan Mantri Jan Dhan Yojana (PMJDY) have made it easier for women to access health care, clean energy, entrepreneurship, and financial freedom (MoPNG, 2022; UNDP, 2022).

Most significantly, the application of 33% reservation in Panchayati Raj Institutions (PRIs) has enabled more than 1.3 million women at grass-root levels to become empowered, promoting governance through further consideration of social concerns such as water, sanitation, and health (Chattopadhyay & Duflo, 2004).Maternal death rates falling to 97 per 100,000 live births in 2022 is shown to be successes in health policy and infrastructure (UNDP, 2022).

These advances notwithstanding, deeply entrenched structural and cultural impediments persist. Wage inequality, employment segregation by occupation, unpaid care work, and workplace safety remain significant constraints on women's involvement in the world of work (GSMA, 2022; OECD, 2021). Even among skilled women, many drop out from work due to the threefold burden of labor, care work, and social expectations.In addition, a mere 33% of rural Indian women have access to mobile internet, which severely limits their ability to enter digital realms and economic opportunity (GSMA, 2022). These patriarchal values of early marriage, preference for sons, and mobility constraint continue to deprive women of agency and autonomy, particularly in rural and conservative locales (Crenshaw, 1989; Kabeer, 1999). Institutionalization of government schemes is weakened by inadequate funding, poor monitoring, and beneficiary ignorance (CAG, 2018; NITI Aayog, 2020). For instance, the Comptroller and Auditor General (CAG) accounted that more than 60% of BBBP money was utilized for media interface, having no significant on-ground effect (CAG, 2018).A real challenge is also political, as women continue to be vastly underrepresented at the higher echelons. Women hold below 15% of seats in the Lok Sabha members (Parliament of India, 2024), and the perpetually pending Women's Reservation Bill reflects perpetual political stagnation towards actual gender equity. Applying feminist theoretical frameworks namely liberal feminism, which advocates equal legal rights; radical feminism, which challenges patriarchal control of institutions; and intersectional feminism, which focuses on the interplaying aspects of discrimination allows for deeper understanding of why the gaps persist (Tong, 2009; Crenshaw, 1989). Empowerment theory (Rappaport, 1981; Zimmerman, 1995) further provides a psychosocial lens through which empowerment is understood not just as an outcome, but as a process of gaining control over one's life.

In conclusion, women's empowerment in India is both a developmental and sociocultural project. Though the country has registered gains in literacy, health, and political participation at the grassroots level, empowerment is still elusive without systemic change. The solution lies in making policy implementation more effective, taking legal literacy to a larger population, inducing behavioral change, and insuring that programs of empowerment touch the most marginalized groups. Efforts in the future will have to transcend symbolic gains and seek to alter the gendered power structures of the country, thus allowing Indian women to exercise full citizenship and autonomy.CAG (2018). Performance Audit on Beti Bachao Beti Padhao Scheme.

References

Chattopadhyay, R., & Duflo, E. (2004). Women as policy makers: Evidence from a randomized policy experiment in India. *Econometrica, 72* (5), 1409-1443. https://onlinelibrary.wiley.com/doi/abs/10.1111/j.1468-0262.2004.00539.x

Comptroller and Auditor General of India (CAG). (2018)*Performance audit of Beti Bachao Beti Padhao Scheme* . https://cag.gov.in/en/audit-report/details/46174

Cornwall, A., & Edwards, J. (2010). Introduction: Negotiating empowerment*IDS Bulletin, 41* (2), 1-9.

https://onlinelibrary.wiley.com/doi/abs/10.1111/j.1759-5436.2010.00117.x

Crenshaw, K. (1989). Demarginalizing the intersection of race and sex: A Black feminist critique of antidiscrimination doctrine, feminist theory and antiracist politics*University of Chicago Legal Forum, 1989* (1), Article 8. https://chicagounbound.uchicago.edu/uclf/vol1989/iss1/8/

GSMA. (2022).*The mobile gender gap report 2022* . https://www.gsma.com/r/wp-content/uploads/2022/06/The-Mobile-Gender-Gap-Report-2022.pdf

Kabeer, N. (1999). Resources, agency, achievements: Reflections on the measurement of women's empowerment*Development and Change, 30* (3), 435-464.

https://onlinelibrary.wiley.com/doi/abs/10.1111/1467-7660.00125

Malhotra, A., Schuler, S. R., & Boender, C. (2002)*Measuring women's empowerment as a variable in international development* . World Bank Gender and Development Group. https://www.academia.edu/17726621/Measuring_womens_empowerment_as_a_variable_in_international_development

Ministry of Finance. (2023)*PM Jan Dhan Yojana progress report* . Government of India.

Ministry of Panchayati Raj. (2022). *Status of elected women representatives in PRIs* . Government of India.

Ministry of Petroleum and Natural Gas (MoPNG). (2022)*Ujjwala Yojana dashboard* . Government of India.

Ministry of Women and Child Development. (2023).*Annual report 2022-2023* . Government of India. https://www.india.gov.in/annual-reports-ministry-women-and-child-development

National Crime Records Bureau (NCRB). (2022).*Crime in India report* . Ministry of Home Affairs. https://ruralindiaonline.org/en/library/resource/crime-in-india-2022-volume-ii/

National Family Health Survey (NFHS-5). (2021).*Fact sheets: India and states* . Ministry of Health and Family Welfare. https://www.mohfw.gov.in/sites/default/files/NFHS-5_Phase-II_0.pdf

NITI Aayog. (2020).*Strategy for New India @75* . Government of India. https://www.niti.gov.in/the-strategy-for-new-india

Nussbaum, M. (2000). *Women and human development: The capabilities approach* . Cambridge University Press. https://www.cambridge.org/core/books/women-and-human-development/58D8D2FBFC1C9E902D648200C4B7009E

OECD. (2021). *Time use across the world: Gender inequality in unpaid work* . Organisation for Economic Co-operation and Development.

Parliament of India. (2024) *Members of the Lok Sabha by gender* . https://www.jagranjosh.com/general-knowledge/members-of-parliament-2024-check-complete-list-here-1717974308-1

Periodic Labour Force Survey (PLFS). (2023). *Annual report 2022-2023* . Ministry of Statistics and Programme Implementation. https://mospi.gov.in/download-reports?main_cat=ODU5&cat=All&sub_category=All

Rappaport, J. (1981). In praise of paradox: A social policy of empowerment over prevention. *American Journal of Community Psychology, 9* (1), 1-25. https://psycnet.apa.org/record/1982-01824-001

Sen, A. (1999)*Development as freedom* . Oxford University Press. http://www.c3l.uni-oldenburg.de/cde/OMDE625/Sen/Sen-intro.pdf

Tong, R. (2009)*Feminist thought: A more comprehensive introduction* (3rd ed.). Westview Press. https://www.taylorfrancis.com/books/mono/10.4324/9780429495243/feminist-thought-rosemarie-tong

United Nations Development Programme (UNDP). (2022). *Human development report 2021/2022: Uncertain times, unsettled lives: Shaping our future in a transforming world* . https://hdr.undp.org/content/human-development-report-2021-22

World Economic Forum. (2024).*Global gender gap report 2024* . https://www.weforum.org/publications/global-gender-gap-report-2024/digest/

Zimmerman, M. A. (1995). Psychological empowerment: Issues and illustrations.*American Journal of Community Psychology, 23* (5), 581-599. https://link.springer.com/article/10.1007/BF02506983

Sarita Mahiwal

इनका नाम सरिता महिवाल है ये हरियाणा से है वर्तमान में ये उत्तर प्रदेश में रहती हैं इन्हें अपने लेखन से लोगों को जागरूक करना अच्छा लगता है ये प्रकृति प्रेमी है और अभी तक 400 से अधिक पेड़ लगा चुकी है ये 100 से अधिक सांझा संग्रह में सहलेखिका रह चुकी हैं ये 2024 में अंतर्राष्ट्रीय कविता प्रतियोगिता में प्रथम स्थान प्राप्त कर चुकी है 26 अगस्त 2024 को इन्हें महिला समानता काव्य रत्न सम्मान से सम्मानित किया गया है साथ ही स्वच्छ भारत अभियान और महिलाओं के जीवन में अंबेडकर के योगदान जैसी प्रतियोगिता में भी इन्हें सम्मानित किया गया है नेपाल की प्रसिद्ध संस्था " शब्द प्रतिभा बहुक्षेत्रीय सम्मान फाउन्डेशन नेपाल " द्वारा नेपाल में बर्ष 2025 में आयोजित किए जाने वाले गौरवशाली सम्मान समारोह " विश्व प्रतिभा अंतरराष्ट्रीय सम्मान समारोह " में " वर्ल्ड टैलेंट इंटरनेशनल अवॉर्ड " के लिए इनका नाम चयन किया गया है। कई न्यूज़ पेपर और पत्रिकाओं में भी इनकी रचनाएं प्रकाशित होती रहती हैं।

हे नारी अपनी प्रतिभा को पहचानों तुम

खुद पर विश्वास जता लो तुम
शिक्षा को हथियार बनाकर
जीवन सुदृढ़ बना लो तुम

कल्पना, इंदिरा, लक्ष्मी बाई,
रणचंडी सारे रूप हो तुम
परचम पूरे विश्व में लहराती
अबला नहीं सबला हो तुम

तुम ही जल में, तुम ही थल में
आकाश में भी पहुंची हो तुम
तोड़ दो सारी जंजीरों को
मंजिल की ओर कदम बढ़ा लो तुम

सुनो.. सुदृढ़ समाज के लिए
जरूरत पड़े तो शमशीर उठा लो तुम

लेकिन जब देखों किसी की पीड़ा
तो मदर टेरेसा खुद को बना लो तुम

शालीनता का आवरण ओढ़ कर
प्रखर विचारों से खुद को सजा लो तुम
जीवन की कठिन से कठिन डगर में
हौसलों को साथी बना लो तुम

किस-किस को क्या समझाओगी?

उठो नारी खुद को सुदृढ़ बनालों,

कब तक गुहार लगाओगी?

छोड़ो मेहंदी खड्ग उठा लो,

कब तक अश्रु बहाओगी?

कल तक जो अंधा था राजा,

अब गूंगा बहरा भी है

अपनी लज्जा आप बचा लो,

कब तक आस लगाओगी?

उनसे रक्षा मांग रही तुम,

जो खुद लज्जाहीन पड़े

वो क्या लाज बचाएंगे,

जो खुद अपराधी के साथ खड़े

नारी होना जुर्म हैं क्या,

ये सोच कब तक घुटती जाओगी?

अपनी आत्म रक्षा की खातिर,

कब तुम कदम उठाओगी?

अति हो गई बर्बरता की,

अब ना तुम विश्राम करो

रणचंडी का रूप धरो तुम,

दुष्टों का संघार करो

उठो नारी अब शस्त्र उठालों,

तनिक ना तुम विलंब करो

छोड़ों बिंदी, छोड़ों गजरा,

लक्ष्मीबाई का रूप धरो

इन नयनों के अश्रु से,

किस-किस को क्या समझाओगी?

न्यायालयों में भटक-भटक कर,

अंतिम आस गवाओगी

कैसे मिलेगा इंसाफ़ तुम्हें,

जब सबके सब हैं मौन पड़े

गलती हो जाती है जवानी में,

कहते, ऐसे नेता सत्ता में खड़े

भय निकाल फेंको अब मन से,

तुम खुद अपना इंसाफ़ करो

कोमलता को ना बना कमजोरी,

तुम खुद पर विश्वास करो

उठो नारी अब शस्त्र उठालों,

कब तक गुहार लगाओगी?

छोड़ो मेहंदी खड्ग उठा लो,

कब तक अश्रु बहाओगी?

Nilofar Farooqui Tauseef

Nilofar Farooqui Tauseef is a distinguished professional and writer hailing from Bihar Sharif, Nalanda, and currently based in Mumbai. With an impressive academic background, she holds both an MCA and an MBA degree. Professionally, she excels as a Project Manager, showcasing her leadership and organizational skills. However, her true passion lies in writing, where she uses her pen as a powerful tool to express her thoughts and emotions, firmly believing that "The pen is a sword to bring revolution."

नारी शक्ति युग-युग में

नारी शक्ति है...., नारी भक्ति है.....,

नारी ही सम्मान है।

उज्जवल धरा के,

तीनो लोक में नारी ही अभिमान है।

जन्म धरे धरती पे...., फिर जननी कहलाये।

हरण हो जब नारी का, काली रूप बन जाये।

नारी दुर्गा है, नारी काली है,

नारी ही आत्मविश्वास है।

नारी ही त्रिनेत्रि, नारी ही शूलधारिणी,

नारी सर्वासुरविनाश है।

माते बनकर चरणो में स्वर्ग लेकर आये।

समय का गिरे प्रकोप, तो चण्डाल भी बन जाये।

नारी सत्या है, नारी सुंदरी है, नारी ही सर्वास्त्रधारिणी है।

नारी लक्ष्मी है, नारी भाविनी है, नारी ही चण्डमुण्ड विनाशिनि है।

नारी शक्ति है..., नारी भक्ति है...., नारी ही सम्मान है।

उज्जवल धरा के, तीनो लोक में नारी ही अभिमान है।

हर युग में नारी ही स्वरुप है।

समानता संग बहुरूप है।

नारीवादी

एक नारी हूँ , स्वंय का अस्तित्व जानती हूँ।

जीवन से मरण तक पहचानती हूँ।

नारीवादी तो किरण है आशावादी की।

समझे न कोई इसे निराशावादी की।

संघर्ष जीवन का हिस्सा है,

हर हिस्से से जुड़ा नारी का किस्सा है।

बहन हो तो भाई साथ जाए, माँ हो तो बेटा,

किसने बनाई ये नीति किसने किसको लुटा।

समाज करे बहिष्कार, फिर अपनाए,

नेता भाषण देकर, वोट बैंक खुलवाए।

आज़ादी हुआ है देश, फिर अब तक हम आज़ाद नहीं।

उन्नति आये कैसे, अशिक्षा क्या करता बर्बाद नहीं।

हर स्थान पे बाँट दिया है नारी के विचार,

हे पुरुषत्मक प्रथा बन्द करो उपकार।

Rohit Jain

Rohit Jain is a forward-thinking educator and advocate for constructivist learning, emphasizing hands-on, inquiry-based education. Passionate about student-centered science education, he works toward refining practical formats for middle school students, ensuring clarity and engagement. Beyond education, Rohit actively supports social justice and women's empowerment, promoting impactful messaging and progressive change. His commitment to equality and innovative teaching methods defines his approach to learning and societal transformation.

Women Empowerment: Breaking Barriers, Shaping Futures

"Feminism is not biological; feminism is an ideology."– Kamala Bhasin

Women empowerment is not merely a concept—it is an urgent call for equality. Women have long been constrained by social norms, relegated to domestic roles, and denied opportunities. However, history is filled with remarkable women who defied conventions and reshaped the world. From Fatima Sheikh, India's first Muslim woman teacher, who fought for education, to scientists like Dr. Archana Sharma and Janaki Ammal, who revolutionized STEM, their stories inspire generations.

Despite progress, gender disparity persists. Women bear the brunt of "time poverty" due to uneven distribution of domestic responsibilities, limiting their career prospects.

We must amplify the voices of women scientists, engineers, educators, and leaders who inspire change. Recognizing and valuing their contributions is essential. As Chief Justice DY Chandrachud aptly put it, "If women want to balance family and career, it is our duty to provide institutional support."

Empowerment means recognizing women's contributions, valuing their labor—both professional and domestic—and ensuring equal opportunities.

Equality is not a privilege; it is a right. Let us celebrate achievements, break stereotypes, and create a world where every woman thrives!

What Can You Do Every Day to Empower Women?

Imagine this: a woman is passed over for a leadership role because "she might not be able to juggle work and home."A young girl hesitates to pursue science because "it's not a field for women."

These biases exist all around us—sometimes in subtle, unspoken ways. But empowerment begins when individuals decide to challenge these narratives.

Here's how you can make an impact in everyday life:

Recognize and Value Women's Work-

Household labor is often dismissed as "labour for love." Acknowledge that domestic work is real work, and advocate for fair recognition and redistribution of responsibilities.

Engage in Meaningful Conversations -

Listen to women's experiences without judgment. Challenge biases—whether in workplace discussions, casual conversations, or social norms.

Support Women's Education and Growth-

Encourage young girls to pursue careers beyond traditional expectations. Education is a powerful tool for dismantling inequality, as Michelle Obama put it, "When girls are educated, their countries become stronger and more prosperous."

Rethink Gender Roles in Parenting -

Childcare is a responsibility, not a burden. Advocate for institutional support that allows women and men to balance family

Celebrate Achievements & Representation-

Recognizing women's contributions in science, technology, and leadership fosters change.

Empowerment isn't a distant goal—it's built through the choices we make daily. How will you contribute today?

Tanveer Sarvar

Tanveer is a passionate writer who enjoys expressing ideas through words and storytelling. With a deep interest in social issues and personal growth, Tanveer uses writing as a tool to inspire and create awareness. Known for thoughtful perspectives and a strong voice, Tanveer continues to explore new themes and share meaningful content with readers

Women Empowerment - A Step Toward Equality, Break The Patriarchy And Stop The Violence

Women Empowerment:

Women empowerment means giving women the freedom to make their own choices, speak up for themselves, and live with respect. It means giving women the same opportunities, rights, and value that men have—in education, at work, in the home, and in society.

For many years, women have been treated unfairly. In many places, girls are not allowed to go to school or work. Many women suffer from violence, harassment, and even abuse—just because they are women. This is wrong and must be stopped. No human being should be treated as less than others because of their gender.

Male Dominated Society:

A major reason behind this unfair treatment is patriarchy—a system where men hold the power and make most of the decisions. In this kind of society, women are often seen as nothing more than house workers, like maids, or as people who are only meant to give birth and care for children. Sadly, many people still believe this is the only role a woman should have.

What's even more painful is that some elderly women with traditional views also continue this thinking. Because they faced these same injustices, they pass them on to the next generation. They do not question the suffering they experienced and expect young girls to accept the same. This cycle must be broken.

Women are strong. If a woman can bring a new life into the world, she has the strength to achieve anything. If given the chance, she can do even better than men in education, business, science, and leadership. We must give every girl the opportunity to grow and shine. But when a woman stands against violence or pursues a career, her own family or partner may refuse support. If she raises her voice or socializes freely, they shame her, questioning her character unfairly.

Peak Of Violence Against Women:

Talking about the violence in some communities, violence against women takes a very cruel form. For example, I read about a practice "Female Genital Mutilation" where, after a girl reaches puberty, or starts her menstruation, her private parts are stitched using old and unclean needles—without any medical care and sanitization. This is done to control her, not to protect her. It causes serious health problems and emotional pain, trauma, and such harmful traditions must end.

High Time To Bring The Change:

To truly bring change, we must start at home. We need to teach our sons that women deserve the same respect as men. Change begins from within. If we are teaching our daughters how to cook or do household chores, we should teach our sons the same. If we ask a girl to sit properly, we must also teach our boys that if a woman is not sitting in a way they like, they should lower their gaze instead of judging her. That is how we create a comfortable and respectful environment where women feel safe and confident.

Conclusion:

In conclusion, women empowerment is not just about helping women—it is about creating a better world for everyone. It is about fairness, respect, and giving every human being the chance to live freely. Let's support every girl and woman, and teach our sons and daughters the true meaning of equality and women empowerment.

Dr. Swati Srivastava

Dr. Swati Srivastava is an Assistant Professor in the School of Management at Babu Banarasi Das University, Lucknow, Uttar Pradesh, India. She specializes in management education and is dedicated to fostering academic excellence and practical learning among her students.

Heart of Our Home :My Maa

In her arms, the world feels right,

A guiding star, my shining light.

Through every storm, through every fall,

She stands beside me, through it all.

Her hands are worn, her heart is wide,

She hides her tears, her pain inside.

With every smile, she lifts my day,

In silent prayers, she lights my way.

She knows us all, each heart, each face,

Bringing warmth to every space.

She loves my father, strong and true,

In her presence, love always grew.

She embraced a family with grace so grand,
Taught us values with a gentle hand.
What joy still to grow in her care,
She shielded us from the world's despair.

Our home where love would stay,
Far from politics and the world's gray.
She loved my brother the very most,
And he is the heart of her own, almost.

When he returned, oh, what a sight—
She cooked his favorites with pure

delight.

She loved my husband like her own son,

Laughing and chatting, what beautiful fun.

Talking cricket, cheering games with glee,

A perfect woman, as perfect could be.

She adored my bhabhi, kind and true,

Doing all the things a good heart would do.

Nevaan, Gaurvee, and little Anay too,

Her grandkids adore her through and through.

Her love is their shelter, joy, and song,

In her company, they feel they belong.

Mumma, O Mumma, you're our soul,

The thread that binds and makes us whole.

We love you more than words can show,

Our heartbeat, our life you need to know.

डॉ शरीफ़ ख़ान

डॉ. शरीफ़ खान, स्नातक (रसायन इंजीनियरिंग) यांत्रिकी अभियांत्रिकी डिप्लोमा, एमबीए (मा. संसाधन), स्नातक (समाज शास्त्र, इतिहास और लोक प्रशासन), स्नातकोत्तर (लोक प्रशा.), विधि स्नातक, स्नातकोत्तर (श्रम कानून, का. प्रबंधन, औद्यो. संबंध) , विद्या वाचस्पति (मानद डॉक्टरेट उपाधि), विद्या सागर (डी लिट.), साहित्य शिरोमणि (विक्रमशिला तथा कशी हिंदी विद्यापीठ), एडवांस डिप्लोमा (उर्दू एवं अरबी).

उपलब्धियां: विभागीय रिकोग्निशन अवार्ड, विशिष्ट योगदान अवॉर्ड,हिंदी सेवी सम्मान (भारत सरकार) राजभाषा भूषण सम्मान. अन्तर्राष्ट्रीय ज्ञान विभूषण सम्मान,धराधाम अंतरराष्ट्रीय व एशिया बुक ऑफ़ वर्ल्ड रिकॉर्ड), शिक्षा रत्न (ग्लोकल युनिवर्सिटी) आदि

"विज्ञान प्रौद्योगिकी में परिवर्तन लाती महिलाएं"

संदर्भ: गूगल नेट से, विभिन्न संदर्भिक आंकड़े आदि।

प्रस्तावना: महिला सशक्तिकरण का अभिप्राय या तात्पर्य है कि महिलाओं को सामाजिक, आर्थिक, शैक्षिक, तकनीकी, कौशलता और राजनैतिक रूप से आत्मनिर्भर बनाना। विज्ञान और तकनीक के क्षेत्र में महिलाओं की भागीदारी इस दिशा में एक अहम कदम है विज्ञान और प्रौद्योगिकी के क्षेत्र में महिलाएं आज न केवल योगदान दे रही हैं, बल्कि वे परिवर्तन की अग्रदूत प्रेरणा दायिनी भी बन चुकी हैं। सदियों से यह क्षेत्र पुरुष प्रधान रहा है, लेकिन अब महिलाएं अपनी बुद्धि, परिश्रम, कुशलता, काबिलियत, सामर्थ्य और नवाचार से इसमें नई ऊर्जा दे रही हैं।

(A). **इतिहास से प्रेरणा**: फ्रैंकलिन, मैडम क्यूरी, कल्पना चावला, सुनीता विलियम जैसी महिलाओं ने यह साबित किया कि विज्ञान क्षेत्र सिर्फ़ पुरुषों का ही मोहताज नहीं है। भारतीय परिप्रेक्ष्य में, टेसी थॉमस, जिन्हें "मिसाइल वूमन ऑफ इंडिया" कहा जाता है, या इसरो ISRO की महिला वैज्ञानिकों की टीम जो चंद्रयान और मंगलयान के प्रोजेक्ट में

प्रमुख भूमिका निभाई थीं, आज ये सभी सराहनीय और प्रेरणा का स्रोत हैं।

(B). **वर्तमान परिदृश्य**: आज भारत ही नहीं बल्कि विश्व भर में महिलाएं कृत्रिम बुद्धिमत्ता (AI), अंतरिक्ष अनुसंधान (space Research), बायोटेक्नोलॉजी, रोबोटिक्स, पर्यावरणीय विज्ञान, और सूचना प्रौद्योगिकी, तकनीकी साहित्य में अग्रणी भूमिका निभा रही हैं। वे न केवल अन्वेषण और अनुसंधान कर रही हैं, बल्कि नए स्टार्टअप शुरू कर रही हैं, शिक्षा, तकनीकी साहित्य में भी नवाचार , नई ऊर्जा ला रही हैं, और समाज के सामने विज्ञान, टेक्नोलॉजी को प्रस्तुत कर रही हैं।

(C). **विज्ञान और प्रौद्योगिकी**: यह किसी भी देश की प्रगति की रीढ़ हैं। जब महिलाएं इस क्षेत्र में सक्रिय रूप से भाग लेती हैं, तो यह न केवल उनके व्यक्तिगत सशक्तिकरण का प्रतीक होता है, बल्कि समाज के समग्र विकास का मार्ग भी प्रशस्त करता है।

(D). **विज्ञान और तकनीक में महिलाओं की भूमिका**: महिलाएं वैज्ञानिक अनुसंधानों, नवाचारों, अंतरिक्ष अभियानों, सूचना प्रौद्योगिकी, बायोटेक्नोलॉजी, आर्टिफिशियल इंटेलिजेंस जैसे क्षेत्रों में महत्वपूर्ण

योगदान दे रही हैं। वे अब केवल प्रयोगशालाओं तक सीमित नहीं हैं, बल्कि संस्थाओं की निदेशक, शोध प्रमुख और नीति निर्धारिक बन रही है।

(E). **महिला वैज्ञानिकों की प्रेरणादायक मिसालें**: डॉ. टेसी थॉमस: भारत की"मिसाइल वूमन" कहलाती हैं एवं डॉ. स्वाति मोहन: नासा के मार्स मिशन की प्रमुख संचालन अधिकारी रहे हैं।

(F). **सरकारी, सामाजिक, संस्थागत पहल**: इसके तहत आज भारत सरकार ने विशेष प्रोत्साहन योजनाएं" — जैसे KIRAN (Knowledge Involvement in Research Advancement through Nurturing), महिलाओं को विज्ञान में आगे बढ़ने के लिए मंच प्रदान करती है, महिला वैज्ञानिक योजना और विज्ञान ज्योति जैसे कई कार्यक्रम चलाए हुए हैं, जो महिलाओं को विज्ञान में आगे बढ़ने के लिए प्रोत्साहित करते हैं। स्कूल स्तर पर भी आज स्टेम STEM (Science, Technology, Engineering, Mathematics) शिक्षा को बढ़ावा देने के लिए विशेष कार्यक्रम चलाए जा रहे हैं।

(G). **विज्ञान में महिला सशक्तिकरण के फ़ायदे**: वैज्ञानिक दृष्टिकोण का विकास, आत्मनिर्भरता और

आत्मविश्वास में वृद्धि,

रोजगार और उद्यमिता के अवसर, लैंगिक समानता को बढ़ावा, सामाजिक विकास में गति इत्यादि।

(H). **चुनौतियाँ और रुकावटें**: अगर रूढ़िवादी सोच के तहत अवसरों की असमानता, कार्यस्थल पर भेदभाव और पारिवारिक दबाव के मुद्दे होंगे, तो महिलाओं की पूर्ण भागीदारी में बाधा बन सकते हैं। हालांकि अब भी सामाजिक मान्यताएं, अवसर की कमी, लैंगिक भेदभाव जैसी समस्याएं महिलाओं को पूरी योग्यता, क्षमता एवं सामर्थ्य से उभरने से रोकती हैं। लेकिन इन बाधाओं के बावजूद महिलाओं के योगदान की उपस्थिति लगातार बढ़ रही है।

उपसंहार: विज्ञान और प्रौद्योगिकी में महिलाओं का सशक्तिकरण केवल उनके उज्जवल भविष्य की नींव ही नहीं रखता, अपितु एक सशक्त, समावेशी और प्रगतिशील समाज की दिशा में सराहनीय, अहम कदम है। महिलाएं प्रयोगशाला से लेकर अंतरिक्ष तक पहुंचती हैं, तो वे दुनिया को एक नया आकार देती हैं, विज्ञान और प्रौद्योगिकी में महिलाएं न केवल भागीदारी अदा करती हैं, बल्कि वे उनकी दशा के साथ दिशा भी तय कर रही हैं। आने वाले

समय में इनका योगदान और भी महत्वपूर्ण होने होगा। हमें न केवल उनकी उपलब्धियों को पहचानना होगा, बल्कि एक ऐसा माहौल भी तैयार करना होगा जिसमें हर लड़की, हर महिला निडर होकर शिक्षाविद् के साथ तकनीकीविद (Technocrate) वैज्ञानिक(scientist) बनने का सपना साकार कर सके।

संदर्भ: विभिन्न संदर्भिक आंकड़े, गूगल नेट से साभार, न्यूज पेपर्स, विभिन्न संदर्भिक क्षेत्रों से जुड़े आंकड़े, नेट से आंकड़े आदि आदि।।

भारत में महिला

प्रधानता व नेतृत्व और इनके

हाथ में शासन सत्ता की बागडोर

प्रस्तावना - कोई भी घर, गांव,

समाज और किसी भी देश का

निर्माण बिना महिलाओं के

संभव ही नहीं है। भारत में

महिला प्रधानता और नेतृत्व

इनके हाथ में शासन सत्ता की

बागडोर सौंपना यह बहुत ही

व्यापक दृष्टिकोण को

दर्शाता है। यह राष्ट्र

निर्माण और उन्नति व विकास के

पथ पर अग्रसर होते हुए विकसित

राष्ट्र में महिलाओं की

पूर्ण राजनीतिक भागीदारी से

संबंधित है। जहां निर्णय

लेने की प्रक्रिया, राजनीतिक

चेतना व समझ आदि के लिए उनकी

जिम्मेदारी सुनिश्चित करने

में संबंधित है। आज हर

क्षेत्र में नारियां अपने दम

पर अपनी पहचान पुख्ता कर रही

है। घर की चारदीवारी से बाहर

की दुनिया में अपनी क्षमता से

सबका ध्यान खींच रही हैं।

वैश्विक दुनिया में सरकार,

व्यवसाय, उच्च शिक्षा,

गैर-लाभकारी उद्यमों और जीवन

के अन्य क्षेत्रों में कई

महिलाएं नेतृत्व क्षमता की

कसौटी पर पुरुषों को कड़ी

टक्कर दे रही हैं। अब नारियों

के लिए कोई भी क्षेत्र अछूता

या अपरिहार्य नहीं रहा।

नाज़ुक, कमजोर और शारीरिक

बनावट का बहाना कहावतों में

ही रह गयी है। समाज की दोहरी

मानसिकता को चुनौती देती

नारी माँ, बहन, पत्नी, बेटी के

रूप में प्रकृति को अपनी ताकत

मान घर की नींव, सृष्टि का

आधार और राष्ट्र ,समाज को आधी

आबादी की महत्ता का इतिहास

समझाती जा रही है, नारी हमारे

समाज की रीढ़ ही नहीं देश का

मान, सम्मान स्वाभिमान भी

हैं। अगर महिला जन

प्रतिनिधित्व की संख्या

ज्यादा होगी, नारी शक्ति आगे

आकर भारत सरकार के साथ कार्य

करने लगेगी, महिलाओं के

उत्थान के लिए नई-नई योजनाएं

ले जाएंगे। भारत की महिलाओं

को मुख्य धारा में लाया

जाएगा, जिससे भारत की महिलाएं

राजनीति में बढ़-चढ़कर

प्रवेश करेगी।

नारी की समाज में स्थिति -

महिला परिवार की एक

महत्वपूर्ण धूरी हैं और

परिवारों का समूह समाज

कहलाता है। वर्तमान युग जन

जागरण का युग हैं जहां नारी

जाति के जागरण की चर्चा

विमर्श स्वाभाविक है।आजादी के इतने वर्षों बाद भी आज महिलाओं की आधी आबादी की स्थिति शोचनीय है। विशेष तौर से अशिक्षिता निम्न व मध्यम वर्गीय महिलाएं आज भी घूंघट के अन्दर अपने अधिकारों से अनभिज्ञ हैं बस अपने कर्तव्यों का बखूबी निर्वहन की और उन्मुख हैं। कहा जाता है कि महिला व पुरुष एक सिक्के के दो पहलू हैं। महिला और पुरुष दोनों ज़िन्दगी रुपी एक गाड़ी के दो पहिए के समान हैं। उक्त कथन दोनों के समान महत्त्व को दर्शाते हैं। सृष्टि की इस सुन्दर रचना में दोनों का महत्व समान

है तो फिर एक को दूसरे से कम
क्यों आंका जाता है? कहावत भी
है अकेला चना भाड़ नहीं फोड़
सकता। सही है राष्ट्र
निर्माण में पुरुषों का ही
नहीं नारी का भी महत्वपूर्ण
उत्तरदायित्व है। नारी
चाहें शिक्षित हो या
अशिक्षित अपने पूरे
आत्मविश्वास के साथ घर
परिवार की सारी जिम्मेदारी
बखूबी निभाती आ रही है तो घर
के बाहर भी अपनी प्रतिभा दमखम
प्रदर्शित कर सकतीं हैं। 1951
में भारत की साक्षरता का दर 18.3%
था। जिसमें केवल 9 प्रतिशत
महिलाएं साक्षर थी। 2021 में

महिला औसत रूप से 77.70 प्रतिशत

साक्षर हुई, पुरुषों का औसत 84.70

% था। ग्रामीण आंचलिक पंचायती

स्तरों पर अधिकांश महिलाओं

को केवल नाम के लिए मुखोटे की

तरह उनका इस्तेमाल किया जाता

है। चुनाव जब आता है, महिलाओं

को चुनाव में खड़ा किया जाता

है, वह चुनाव तो लड़ती है जीत

भी जाती है, लेकिन सत्ता

पुरुष ही संभालते हैं। सभी

निर्णय पुरुष ही लेते है, यह

वास्तविकता आज भी पंचायत

राज्यों में देखने के लिए मिल

रही है। क्योंकि महिलाएं

अशिक्षित है, वह पढ़ी-लिखी

नहीं है ।

महिलाओं की स्थिति का अवलोकन:

आज के परिप्रेश्य में

महिलाओं को आबादी के हिसाब से

(प्रतिशतता में) सत्ता में

प्रधान या मुख्य नेतृत्व

कर्ता के रूप में कोई

खास/विशेष स्थान नहीं दिया

गया है। चूंकि शताब्दियों से

अन्याय व अत्याचार की चक्की

में पिसी जाती हुई नारी आज

अज्ञानता के घूंघट को उलट

दिया है।अपने अधिकारों के

प्रति सजग हुई है और ये सब

शिक्षा के कारण ही संभव हुआ

है। डा. बी.आर.आम्वेडर जी ने

शिक्षा को शेरनी का दूध कहा

है। उन्होंने कहा था "नारी

राष्ट्र की निर्मात्री है, हर

नागरिक उसकी गोद में पलकर

बढ़ता है नारी को जागृत किये

बिना राष्ट्र का विकास संभव

नहीं है।" वे महिलाओं को

संवैधानिक अधिकार दिलाने के

पक्षधर थे। महिलाओं को खुद

समझने की जरूरत है कि अपने

अधिकार और कर्तव्य क्या हैं?

एक सफल नेतृत्व क्षमता उसी

में होती है जो अपने

संवैधानिक अधिकारों के साथ

साथ अपने मूल कर्तव्यों को भी

समझते हुए आगे बढ़े। आधुनिक

भारतीय समाज पुरुष प्रधान

समाज है, इसलिए नारी को कमतर

आंका जाता है; जबकि आदिकाल

में नारी की अग्रणी भूमिका

रही है।

राजनीति में नारी की

सक्रियता: आजकल महिलाएं कई

क्षेत्रों में नेतृत्व का

कार्य पूरी तन्मयता तथा

ईमानदारी के साथ निभा रहीं

हैं। आज भारत में संवैधानिक

अधिकारों के बावजूद राजनीति

में महिलाओं की भागीदारी का

प्रतिशत बहुत कम हैं। इस

विषमता को मिटाने व महिला

सशक्तिकरण के लिए भारतीय

संविधान के 73 वें संशोधन के

आधार पर पंचायती राज

संस्थाओं में महिलाओं,

अनुसूचित जाति, जनजाति एवं

अल्पसंख्यक समुदायों के लिए

सीटें आरक्षित करने की बात

कही गई हैं। जिसके कारण

स्थानीय संस्थाओं में

महिलाओं की सक्रियता बढ़ी है

किन्तु संसद, राज्य

विधानसभाओं में पर्याप्त

संख्या में सहभागिता नहीं

है। भारत के संसदीय इतिहास

में महिला आरक्षण को लेकर

काफी लंबा सफर तय करना पड़ा

और अंततः 33% आरक्षण के साथ

महिलाओं की राजनीति में

भागीदारी सुनिश्चित की गई

है। इस सफर में अनेक बाधायें

आई जो राष्ट्र निर्माण में
महिलाओं की भूमिका को कमतर और
कमज़ोर आंकते रहें। यह हमारे
मौजूदा पुरुष प्रधान
सामाजिक ताने बाने द्वारा
अनेक प्रकार की चुनौतियां
सामने आती रहीं हैं। गृह
कार्य, बच्चों की देखभाल,
लिंग भेद, महिलाओं को चार
दिवारी में रखना, सिर्फ नारी
होने के कारण बुद्धि और
योग्यता को कमतर आंकना,
लैंगिक असमानता, यौन शोषण की
आशंका, आर्थिक स्थिति
सामाजिक स्थिति आदि के कारण
महिलाओं को राजनीति से दूर
रहना पड़ता है। बहुत कम

महिलाएं राजनीति में सक्रिय

भूमिका निभाने में सक्षम

हैं। विशेष रूप से राजपरिवार

की महिलाएं, सेलीब्रिटीज या

राजनीतिक पार्टियों से

जुड़ी हुई कुछ महिलाएं

स्वतंत्र रूप से राजनीतिक

भागीदारी निभा पाते हैं। कई

बार ऐसा देखने में आता है

महिलाएं प्रमुख प्रधान के पद

पर कार्यरत होने के बावजूद

उनके पति या परिवार के पुरूष

सदस्यों द्वारा ही सारे

निर्णय लिया जाता है खास कर

पंचायती व्यवस्था में यह बात

सामने आती हैं। सिर्फ

कठपुतली बन कर रह जाती हैं।

और आम आदमी जो दो समय के लिए ही

भोजन जुटाने में लगा रहता है
उसे राजनीति से कोई सारोकार
नहीं होता।

आधुनिक युग की नारी– आज

आधुनिक नारी अपने मानसिक व
बौद्धिक क्षमता से मंथन कर
सतत् संघर्ष करते हुए
पुरुषों के साथ कंधे से कंधा
मिला कर चल रही हैं। हर
क्षेत्र में बढ़-चढ़ कर
प्रतिभाग कर रही हैं। जिसे
कभी चूल्हे -चौके और घरेलु
कामकाज से मुक्ति नहीं मिलती
थी, आज वह सीमा पर डटी हुई हैं
एवं पाइलेट बन जहाज़, वायुयान
उड़ा रही है। और अंतरिक्ष तक

अपने कामयाबी के परचम लहरा

रही हैं। ज्ञान-विज्ञान,

सामाजिक, सांस्कृतिक, आर्थिक

धार्मिक, राजनीतिक, खेलकूद,

साहित्यिक, चिकित्सा आदि हर

क्षेत्र में अपने आपको

स्थापित कर रही हैं। यह सब

संवैधानिक अधिकारों के

बदौलत संभव हो रहा है।

निःसंदेह नारी में ज्ञान

कौशल, बुद्धिमता, नेतृत्व

क्षमता में कही कोई कमी नहीं

है, कमी है तो सिर्फ अवसर की

समानता और अधिकारों की बात

है। वैसे इतिहास गवाह है कि

पूर्व में भी अनेक महिलाएँ कई

महत्वपूर्ण पदों पर प्रधान

के रूप में अपनी

जिम्मेदारियां बखूबी

निभायीं हैं। चाहे वो

राजनीति हो या फिर औद्योगिक

अन्य किसी भी क्षेत्र की बात

करें, घर परिवार के साथ-साथ

अपने हर कार्य क्षेत्र में

दोहरी जिम्मेदारियां पूरी

तरह तन्मयता के साथ निभाते

हुए कर्तव्य पथ पर सतत् आगे

बढ़ रहीं हैं। केवल भारत ही

नहीं विश्व पटल पर भी अनेक

देशों मे महिलाएं विभिन्न

क्षेत्रों में अपनी

महत्वपूर्ण भूमिका निभा रही

है।

नारी का प्राचीन और अर्वाचीन

इतिहासः नारी शक्ति की गाथा

प्राचीन समय से लेकर वर्तमान
युग तक संघर्ष की गाथा रहीं
हैं। परंतु वैदिक युग के
स्त्री समाज में सती और जौहर
की प्रथा व्यापक रूप से
व्याप्त थी। युद्ध में हार
जाने पर पत्नियाँ पति के साथ
सती हो जाती थीं अथवा सामूहिक
रूप से जौहर कर लेती थीं।
हांडी रानी जैसी कई पत्नियाँ
तो युद्ध में जाते समय झिझक
एवं मोह दिखाने वाले पतियों
के सम्मुख अपना सिर काटकर रख
दिया करती थीं। अतः पुरुष
प्रधान समाज में पल-पल
चुनौतियां मिलीं हैं, नारी

अपने आत्मविश्वास व हौसलों

के साथ सारी बाधाओं को पार

करते हुए निरंतर आगे बढ़ रहीं

हैं। समाज व राष्ट्र के विकास

में सत्ता में प्रधान के रूप

में महिलाएं अपनी भागीदारी

निभा सकती हैं और उन्हें अवसर

मिलना चाहिए। निःसंदेह घर

संसार की तरह राष्ट्र को भी

अवश्य संभालेंगी और राष्ट्र

के उन्नति व विकास में अपना

योगदान दे सकेंगी। उदाहरण

स्वरुप: वीरता अदम्य सहस की

प्रतिमूर्ति झांसी की रानी

लक्ष्मीबाई, बाई, रानी

दुर्गावती है और दूसरी ओर

शिक्षा के क्षेत्र में

विद्या की सावित्रीबाई फुले

जिन्होंने महिलाओं एवं

बालिकाओं के लिए अनेक

विद्यालय खोलें, समाज के घोर

विरोध व अपमान के बावजूद अपने

कर्तव्य पथ से कभी नहीं

डिगीं। इतिहास को उठा कर देखा

जाए तो महिलाओं की योग्यता और

वीरता के किस्से देखने को

मिलते हैं। इसके अतिरिक्त और

भी महिलाएं रहीं हैं

जिन्होंने पुरुषों के साथ हर

क्षेत्र में कंधे से कन्धा

मिलाकर काम किया है। जिनमे

गार्गी, अपाला मराठा महारानी

ताराबाई, घोषा, रत्नावली आदि

नाम प्रसिद्ध हैं। बेगम हजरत

महल, जस्टिस फातिमा, सानिया
मिर्ज़ा आदि ऐतिहासिक
व्यक्तित्व रहे हैं जो हमारे
प्रेरणास्रोत हैं। वही
इतिहास में आदरणीया सरोजिनी
नायडू, श्रीमती इंदिरा गांधी,
पूर्व राष्ट्रपति श्रीमती
प्रतिभा पाटिल, श्रीमती
सुषमा स्वराज, श्रीमती शीला
दीक्षित, श्रीमती निर्मला
सीतारमण, श्रीमती सोनिया
गांधी, सुश्री मायावती,
वर्तमान राष्ट्रपति श्रीमती
द्रौपदी मुर्मू आदि अन्य
अनेकानेक महिलाओं ने
राजनीति के क्षेत्र में
महत्वपूर्ण पदों पर सुशोभित

होकर अपना लोहा मनवा चुकीं

हैं और अब भी कार्यरत है।

महिलाओं की संविधान में

स्थिति और महिला नेतृत्व की

नई क्रांति का आगाज: आजादी के

अमृत महोत्सव पर भी राजनीति

में महिलाओ की भागीदारी हेतु

केवल 33% सीटें आरक्षित हो पाई

है। यहां स्त्री व पुरुषों के

मध्य कोई प्रतिस्पर्धा नहीं

है बात समान प्रतिनिधित्व की

है। चूंकि भारतीय संविधान के

के अनुच्छेद-14 में कहा गया है

कि कानून के सामने स्त्री और

पुरुष दोनों बराबर है।

अनुच्छेद-15 महिलाओं को

भेदभाव के विरुद्ध न्याय का

अधिकार प्रदान करता है। यथा

"राज्य किसी भी नागरिक के

विरुद्ध केवल धर्म,मूलवंश,

जाति, लिंग, जन्म स्थान अथवा

इनमें से किसी आधार पर कोई

विभेद नहीं करेगा।" साथ ही

प्रजातंत्र के समुचित काम

काज के लिए सभी स्तरों पर

सत्ता, निर्णय लेने और

नेतृत्व तक पुरुषों और

महिलाओं की भागीदारी

सुनिश्चित करता है। यानि

महिलाएं अधिक संख्या में

सरकार में शामिल होकर समाज व

राष्ट्र निर्माण,

नीति-निर्धारण महिला हितों

की रक्षा एवं राजनीतिक

मामलों आदि में पारदर्शिता

और जबाबदेही के साथ कर्तव्य

निवर्हन कर सकती है। 1992 में 73

वां और 74 वां विधेयक संशोधन

किया गया, और पंचायत में एक

तिहाई आरक्षण विधेयक पास

किया गया। 33% आरक्षण का प्रयोग

भारत में सबसे पहले पंचायती

राज्य में किया गया। वर्तमान

की स्थिति अगर जाने तो लोकसभा

संसद में 543 सीटों में केवल 15%

महिलाएं यानी की 78 महिलाएं

हमारे सांसद है। राज्यसभा की

स्थिति भी उसे कम ही है, केवल 14%

महिलाएं सत्ता पर बैठी हुई

है। राज्य विधानसभा में तो

केवल 10% महिलाएं ही कार्यरत

है। भारतीय समाज महिलाओं के

बारे में सकारात्मक सोच रखे

उन्हें आगे बढ़ने का सुअवसर

देना चाहिए। लेकिन

संवेधानिक रूप से शासन सत्ता

की बागडोर को सौंपना, नारियों

को प्रधान के रूप में स्वीकार

करना, हमारे देश में पुरुष

प्रधान सामाजिक ताने-बाने

में जकड़ी बेडियों को तोड़कर

उनके अस्तित्व को महत्ता

देते हुए यह गौरवशाली सम्मान

देना,राष्ट्र निर्माण में

महिलाओं की भागीदारी

सुनिश्चित करना सचमुच एक

साहसिक एवं ऐतिहासिक कार्य

है। यह एक नये युग की एक नई
क्रांति का आगाज होगा।

 महिला प्रधानता और नेतृत्व
का विभिन्न क्षेत्रों में
प्रभाव: पहले गांव में महिला
प्रधान तो चुन ली जाती थी
लेकिन बाकी के काम पुरुषों
के द्वारा ही किए जाते थे।
लेकिन फिर देखा गया कि जिस
जगह महिला प्रधान, महिला
शिक्षक, महिला चिकित्सक हैं
वहां कार्य करने में ज्यादा
से ज्यादा सफलता प्राप्त हुई
कि जब एक महिला दूसरी महिला
के संपर्क में आती है तो वह
अपने को सहज महसूस करते हुए
आगे बढ़ती है। महिलाओं को

शासन सत्ता की बागडोर

सौंपनें से निःसन्देह देश की

राजनीति में काफी बदलाव

आयेगा। आर्थिक, सामाजिक

धार्मिक,राजनीतिक, शिक्षा,

चिकित्सा आदि अनेक

क्षेत्रों में भी नए नए अवसर

उपलब्ध होगें। राजनीति में

सक्रिय महिलाओं के कुशल

मार्गदर्शन में विकास के नये

आयाम गढ़े जाएंगे। जो अन्य

महिलाओं के लिए प्रेरणा

स्रोत बनेंगे। महिला और

पुरुष आपस में मिलकर राष्ट्र

की उन्नति, उत्थान के लिए

कार्य करेंगे जो विश्व पटल

पर अपनी अलग पहचान बनायेगें।

जिस प्रकार से स्त्री व
पुरुष घर परिवार में आपसी
सामंजस्य से घर में खुशहाली
लाते हैं और समाज में अपनी
अलग छाप छोड़ते हैं। ऐसे ही
राष्ट्र के संपूर्ण विकास
में कोई कसर नहीं छोड़ेंगे।
ऐसा नहीं कि राष्ट्र विकास
के पथ पर अग्रसर नहीं है,
चूंकि बात महिलाओं को
राजनीति में उचित अवसर मिलने
की है। राजनीति दलों में
महिलाओं की भागीदारी बहुत कम
है। महिलाओं के हाथ में शासन
सत्ता की बागडोर होने से
विश्व व भारत में अनेक बदलाव
देखने को मिलेंगे।
लोकतंत्रात्मक व्यवस्था

में महिला अधिकारिता,

राजनीतिक प्रक्रिया के

विकास में एक अनिवार्य कदम

है। इसका मुख्य उददेश्य

महिलाओं को राजनीति की मुख्य

धारा में लाना है और उन्हें

किसी भी प्रकार के प्रतिबन्ध

व अलगाव से मुक्ति दिलाना

है। महिलाओं को राजनीतिक

अधिकार प्रदान किये जाने की

परिकल्पना उनके उत्थान के

लिए और लैंगिक असमानता तथा

भेदभाव उन्मूलन हेतु एक

सशक्त एवं अनिवार्य माध्यम

के रूप में की गई है। इसके

अनुसरण में भारत का संविधान

महिलाओं को राजनैतिक

अधिकारों की अनिवार्य

निश्चितता प्रदान करता है।

पहले की तुलना में आज कहीं

अधिक महिलाएं दृश्यमान

नेतृत्व प्रदान कर रही हैं।

महिलाओं को एक तिहाई आरक्षण

एक नजर: महिला आरक्षण पर एक

नजर डाले तो भारत के लोकसभा

और राज्यसभा में 33% महिलाओं को

आरक्षण देना यह प्रावधान है।

अर्थात लोकसभा और राज्यसभा

की तीसरी व्यक्ति यह महिला

होगी, इस प्रकार का प्रावधान

महिला आरक्षण विधेयक में रखा

गया है । अर्थात आज वर्तमान

में लोकसभा के 543 सींटों में

से 82 सीटों की जगह पर 181 सीटों

पर महिलाएं सदस्य ही होगी। इस

बिल का इतिहास में सबसे पहले

एच डी देवे गौड़ा की सरकार ने

1996 में इसे पेश किया गया था,

लेकिन तब यह बिल पास नहीं हुआ,

उसके बाद बहुत सारे तमाम

सरकारों ने इसे कानून का रूप

देने का प्रयास किया गया,

लेकिन यह बिल 27 वर्ष तक लटका

रहा। आखिर इसे 128 वें संविधान

संशोधन विधेयक के तहत इसे पेश

किया गया। हमारे भारत के

केंद्रीय कानून मंत्री

अर्जुन राम मेघवालजी ने इस

बिल को "नारी शक्ति अधिनियम"

नाम देकर पेश किया गया। यह

विधेयक 2026 से लागू होगा। भारत

में यह विधेयक लागू होने के

बाद 15 वर्ष तक आरक्षण का प्रभाव रहेगा, इसके बाद सीटों का आवंटन रोस्टर प्रणाली के तहत किया जाएगा। भारतीय संसद में केवल 14 फ़ीसदी महिलाएं देखने को मिलती है। वैश्विक औसत भागीदारी देखा जाए तो 25 फ़ीसदी महिलाएं भारत की देखी जा सकती है।

महिला आरक्षण विधेयक पास करने का और महिलाओं को 33% आरक्षण का मुख्य अर्थ यह है कि, भारत के लोकसभा संसद पदों पर और राज्यसभा की संसद पदों पर एक तिहाई महिलाएं ही हो। भारत की लोकसभा के कुल सीटों

में 33% सीट पर महिला आरक्षण जिसको एक तिहाई आरक्षण कहा जाता है। अर्थात वर्तमान में लोकसभा की 543 सीटों में 33% सीटों पर महिलाएं हो जिसमें SC, ST, OBC महिलाओं का समावेश किया जाए। महिला आरक्षण यह कल्पना सबसे पहले कौन की थी? सन 1931 में सरोजिनी नायडू ने सबसे पहले यह आरक्षण का विचार रखा था, की महिलाओं को आरक्षण देना चाहिए, वह भारत के राजनीति में बहुत ही पीछे है, उसे आगे लाना चाहिए, लेकिन जब यह विधेयक पास नहीं हो पाया। यह विधेयक लागू होने के बाद क्या

परिवर्तन आएगा, महिला विधेयक

दोनों सदनों में पास होकर

राष्ट्रपति के हस्ताक्षर के

बाद, जब इसे देश में लागू किया

जाएगा तो देश के राजनीति में

बहुत बड़ा परिवर्तन आ जाएगा।

उपसंहार– भारत में सदियों से

चली आ रही पितृ सत्तात्मक

व्यवस्था के चलते मातृशक्ति

की पहचान खो सी गई थी। । यदि

सही रूप में देखा जाए तो जिस

घर में महिलाओं को बराबरी का

अधिकार दिया जाता है तो वहां

सभी कार्य कुशलता पूर्वक

सम्पन्न होते हैं। पुरातन

परम्पराओं व रीतिरिवाजों के

चलते घूंघट के ओट में घूंट

घूंट कर जी रही थी । अपने ही घर
में कैद होकर रह गई थी। महिला
घर बाहर कहीं भी सुरक्षित
नहीं थी और अब भी नहीं है। फिर
भी आज महिलाओं व पुरुषों की
मानसिकता उनके नैतिक
मूल्यों में बहुत परिवर्तन
आया है। महिला पुरुष दोनों
साथ-साथ कार्य कर रहे हैं।

स्त्री पुरुष दोनों एक दूसरे
के प्रतिस्पर्धी न होकर
सहयोगी बन कर राष्ट्र
निर्माण में अपना योगदान दे
रहे हैं। विश्व स्तर पर भी
अनेक देशों में महिलाएं
प्रधान की भूमिका निभाती आ
रही हैं। लेकिन भारत देश में
जहां महिलाओ की आधी आबादी

विकास के लिए संघर्ष कर रही
हैं वहां ऐसी परिकल्पना कि
राजनीति में महिलाओं की शत्-
प्रतिशत भागीदारी एवं शासन
सत्ता की बागडोर यदि नारी के
हाथ में हो वास्तव में यह
बहुत बड़ा कदम है ऐसी सोच
प्रशंशनीय है। ऐसे ही स्त्री
पुरुष प्रतिद्वंद्वी नहीं
बल्कि सहयोगी बन कर कर्तव्य
पथ पर साथ-साथ चलेंगे,
निःसंदेह देश में एक नया
इतिहास रचेंगे। जहां समता,
विश्व बंधुत्व, दया, करूणा और
मानवता सर्वोपरि होगा। मैं
इन वास्तविक संकलित
पंक्तियों से अपने इस आलेख को

विराम देता हूँ। कि

भूल करो न समझ के अबला, वो शोला

चिंगारी है,

अत्याचारी के जीवन में, काल

कृपाण कटारी है ।

जितनी नारी दिखती शीतल, मन

में जलती ज्वाला है,

गर मन में कुछ भेद उपजते,

भड़की बन चिंगारी है।

नारी दुर्गा, लक्ष्मी बाई,

सदा समर्पित शौर्या है,

उसको समझ न लेना बेबस, ना सोचो

लाचारी है।

गर सम्मान करोगे उसका, वो

सृष्टि मनोहारी है,

हल्के में मत लो नारी को, नारी

सब पर भारी है।

नारी है नारी को समझो, वो

सम्मानित सत्कारी है,

नारी से है जग की शोभा, घर-घर

में खुशहाली है ।।

Rahul Raikwar

Rahul Raikwar is an experienced English educator with over 9 years of teaching expertise. He is currently serving as the Associate Head of the English Department at Sagar Public School, Bhopal. Known for his passion for language, literature, and innovative pedagogy, he is dedicated to nurturing confident and articulate learners.

A Real Woman: Not a goddess, just a human

There is a dish in China where, the moment a chicken hatches from the egg, it is put in a wooden case and fed dry fruits. When it becomes big enough for that case, it is moved to a bigger one, and rich food continues. The chicken grows up completely inside a case, well-fed, but it never moves. Its bones never form. It becomes large, full of extra fat, but spineless. Then it is cooked. This is how we bring up our daughters. We don't let them have bones.

In today's world, it is still very difficult to find the true definition of an empowered woman. We speak of empowerment, but do we allow girls to grow into strong individuals with their own identity, or do we keep them in metaphorical boxes, feeding them comfort but denying them strength?

This world gives a very special status to a mother, but fails to understand, whose mother? Mine, or my children's? We tend to give respect and status to a woman based on our needs, not her own worth. According to most religions, women are still considered secondary. One example is marriage, a centuries-old tradition that continues to shape women's lives.

Marriage is like a stone that has been rolling down the mountains for generations. As it rolls, it collects moss. Traditions and customs that were originally meant to define the bond but have now turned into restrictions, many of which aim to suppress women. Today, marriage has taken a form that often limits women instead of supporting them.

In my opinion, marriage should be about partnership. It should mean whether the husband and wife are friends with each other, whether they respect each other, and whether there is mutual understanding. Sadly, we talk about gender equality without fully understanding what it really means. Even God has not made men and women exactly the same. He kept some differences,and rightly so.

Women are far more responsible than men in many ways. She is the thread that holds all the pearls together and forms the beautiful necklace that we call a happy family. We, as a society, must understand that both men and women have different roles, and both roles are important.

Gone are the days, when women were called *"**Traditional Sati-Savitri**" or *"Adarsh Bhartiya Naari"*.This is the time when everyone, including women themselves, must understand the true meaning of a modern woman. We must understand their growth, their changing roles, and their journey of evolution.

Women empowerment means giving women the freedom to make their own choices, access to equal opportunities, and the respect to live with dignity in both personal and professional spaces. It is not about making women like men, but about valuing their roles, supporting their growth, and ensuring their voices are heard in every aspect of life. True empowerment begins when we raise daughters to be strong in thought, confident in action, and free from imposed limitations.

When there is less to see, it gives us an eye to see more in less. Do not treat her like a goddess. Treat her like a human being, and give her all the rights that every human deserves. Everyone is human, and she is no different.

Dr Parul Yadav

Parul has a great interest in literature and enjoys writing prose in Hindi. With a deep appreciation for language and storytelling, she often explores cultural and emotional themes through her work, capturing the nuances of everyday life with sensitivity and insight.

विद्रोह करती लड़कियाँ

विद्रोह करती लड़कियाँ, अखरती हैं आँखों में विद्रोह प्रतीक है क्रांति का । विद्रोह करती लड़कियाँ लाती हैं, क्रांति। लोगों को पसंद हैं आवाज़ विहीन लड़कियाँ.. विद्रोह करती लड़कियाँ बोलती हैं अपनी आवाज़ में .. और डरती नहीं ज़रा। विद्रोह करती लड़कियाँ, होती हैं साहसी.. जो लड़ती हैं दमन के ख़िलाफ़ । उठाती हैं कलम, खोलती हैं किताबें, करती हैं सवाल। माँगती हैं तुम्हारे बनाए हुए खोखले, दक़ियानूसी, फ़र्ज़ी और दोहरे चरित्र वाले समाज से जवाब .. जो करता है फ़र्क़ हम औरतों के अलग- अलग किरदारों में । समाज जिसमें शामिल है सभी औरत-आदमी । आज़ादी एक विचार है .. जो सबमें हों ज़रूरी नहीं। विद्रोह करती लड़कियाँ, होती हैं आज़ाद ख़याल, जो देती है टीस, इस क़ैद-पसंद दुनिया को । विद्रोह करती लड़कियाँ, माँगती नहीं 'इजाज़त', देती नहीं हक़ किसी को 'अनुमति' देने का ..लेती हैं अपने फ़ैसले ख़ुद, खटकती हैं इस क़ैद-पसंद समाज को। विद्रोह करती लड़कियाँ होती हैं ख़ूबसूरत, बेहद क्योंकि वो देखती हैं ख़ुद को ख़ुद के चश्मे से ।

और ये एक सतत चलने वाली प्रक्रिया है। विद्रोह तो होगा । क्रांति तो आएगी .. भ्रम तो टूटेगा प्रभुत्व का । और ये होगा। निश्चित ही ।

ख़ूबसूरत लड़कियाँ।

कितनी ख़ूबसूरत होती होंगी वो लड़कियाँ।

जो ढूँढती होंगी नये शहरों में घर..

कितनी ख़ूबसूरत होती होंगी वो लड़कियाँ।

जो करती होंगी अपने पैसों का हिसाब किताब..

कितनी ख़ूबसूरत होती होंगी वो लड़कियाँ।

जो करती होंगी ज़िद, अपनी ज़िद पूरी करने के लिए..

कितनी ख़ूबसूरत होती होंगी वो लड़कियाँ।

जो रखती होंगी हौसला ..सपने देखने का ..

लड़ने का और उसे पूरा करने का

कितनी ख़ूबसूरत होती होंगी वो लड़कियाँ।

जो खाती होंगी धक्के .. सड़कों, बसों, मेट्रो और ट्रेनों में..

कितनी ख़ूबसूरत होती होंगी वो लड़कियाँ।

जिनके हाथों ने सिर्फ़ रोटियाँ नहीं बेली बल्कि
पकड़ी कलम..लिखी अपनी क़िस्मत ..

कितनी ख़ूबसूरत होती होंगी वो लड़कियाँ।

जो अपने प्रेमी से चाहती होंगी तो सिर्फ़ और सिर्फ़ मोहब्बत

नहीं चाहती होगी कोई तोहफ़ा।

चाहती होगी अपने पिता का साया और आशीर्वाद

नहीं चाहती होगी कोई सहारा ..

जो बनना चाहती होगी माँ- बाप का सहारा ।

नहीं चाहती होगी बनना भाई- बहन पर बोझ ।

संग चाहती होगी बोझ बाँटना ..

सच कितनी ख़ूबसूरत होती होंगी ना वो लड़कियाँ!!

डॉ नीलू समीर

डॉ. नीलू शुक्ला समीर एक शिक्षाविद, कवियित्री, संपादक एवं लेखिका हैं। वे 'बुंदेलखंड पब्लिकेशन हाऊस' के साथ एडीटर के रूप में लम्बे समय तक जुड़ी रही हैं। वे सैफिया कॉलेज ऑफ एजुकेशन में प्राचार्या के पद पर रह चुकी हैं एवं देश के विभिन्न महाविद्यालयों में सहायक प्राध्यापक के पद को सुशोभित कर चुकी हैं। वर्तमान में मध्यप्रदेश शासन में अंग्रेजी विषय की ग्रेड 1 की शिक्षिका हैं। अनेक काव्य प्रतियोगिताओ में जज रह चुकी हैं। 'दैनिक विनय उजाला', 'न्यूज धमाका झारखंड' एवं 'साप्ताहिक अमृत राजस्थान' में उनकी रचनाएँ प्रकाशित होती रहती हैं। 2023 में शृंगार रस पर आधारित कविताओं का उनका काव्य संग्रह अन्तर्वीथिका(पुस्तक का विमोचन मध्य प्रदेश साहित्य अकादमी द्वारा हुआ) ,बीहड़ पथ प्रकाशित हो चुका है।

मैं_आत्ममुग्धा

तुम क्या जानोगे मेरी उपलब्धियों को
हाँ हूँ मैं आत्ममुग्धा, हूँ आत्मप्रशंसक
पढ़ते हुए चाय नहीं मिली माँ के हाथों
माँजी को चाय देकर पढ़ाई की है

यम्मी टिफ़िन लेकर नहीं गई कॉलेज
संयुक्त परिवार का खाना बनाकर गई
नाखूनों में पॉलिश नहीं आटा लगा होता
जानी जाती लेट जाने, जल्दी आने हेतु
टीचर कहती, "कैसे होगा गेन नॉलेज"

चोरी किया करती अक्सर समय की
छुपकर पढ़ाई का काम निपटा लेती
टीवी के रिमोट का फंक्शन नहीं जानती
"टेक्नोलॉजी में शून्य" सुनकर हँस लेती

हाँ एमएससी किया है कम्प्यूटर में

किंतु नहीं था कंप्यूटर पर बैठने का समय

परीक्षा वाले दिन किसी को गुस्सा आ जाए

तो कॉपी किताबें भी फाड़ कर फेंक दें

मुस्कराकर बिन पढ़े ही एग्जाम दे आती

लिख आती "अनुभव-स्मृति आधारित"

को-करिकुलर एक्टिविटीज़ में भी आगे

झूठ बोल बोल कर भाग लेना और

हाँ ...ये क्या...ये तालियों की गड़गड़ाहट

सचमुच !! मेरे लिए !! सपना तो नहीं कोई

"मैंने टॉप किया".. उद्घोषणा झूठ तो नहीं।

ये इतनी बड़ी सी ट्रॉफ़ी.. सचमुच मेरी है

जिन टीचर्स की नज़र में "अनियमित छात्रा"

क्या वही मंच से पढ़ रही हैं कसीदे????

जो भी हो... मेरे लिए बहुत बड़ी हैं ये उपलब्धियाँ.....

बड़े सीज़ेरियन ऑपरेशन के दो दिन बाद

इंटरव्यू देने जाना, आँखों के आगे अँधेरा

बेहोशी सी हालत में दिन भर बारी का इंतज़ार

और फिर बड़े - बड़े विशेषज्ञों के प्रश्नों के उत्तर देना

परिणाम.... अविश्वसनीय... क्या सचमुच सेलेक्शन?

ज़रा लिस्ट तो देखूँ..... वो भी फर्स्ट पोजीशन में!!!

ख़ुद की पीठ थपथपाई,"वाकई बहुत बड़ी है ये उपलब्धि मेरे लिए"

छोटे बच्चे को रात भर देखना, बिना सोए ही सुबह काम पर जाना...

सबके उलाहने सुन, दिन-रात सिर्फ़ अपनी कमियाँ सुन

सबको ख़ुश रखने की रात-दिन नाकाम कोशिशें करना

संज्ञा "कमज़ोर" की जगह "कामचोर" की मुस्कराकर सुनना

अपनी प्रशंसा स्वयं से स्वयं कर ख़ुश होते रहना

बात करूँ सौंदर्य की तो तुम क्या जानो इसका रहस्य

दिन-रात अपनी आत्मा को रक्ततप्त कर चमकाया

चेहरे की सफ़ेदी आत्मा की धवलता का रिफ्लेक्शन

आँखों का काजल, रातों को जागना पढ़ने के लिए

होंठों की लाली, खाकर लोगों की गाली, क्रोध को होंठों पर ही रोक लेना

कैसे कर पाएगा कोई इस अप्रतिम सौंदर्य की बराबरी

आजीवन अपनी विनम्रता से सबसे छोटा बना रहना

क्यों नहीं दिखूँ फिर यंग सबसे ज़्यादा सखियों में???

जीवन भर माँ सरस्वती की उपासना में लगे रहना

तो क्यों न हो फिर ज्ञान की सरिताएँ सतत् प्रवाहित

जीवन बने तपस्या करते हुए विपश्यना तो क्यूँ न

कहूँ?

"हूँ मैं विशेष, परिश्रम किया अशेष" बुरा क्यों तुम्हें लगे

"क्यों हूँ मैं आत्ममुग्धा, हाँ क्यों हूँ मैं चिरदग्धा???"

-

www.ingramcontent.com/pod-product-compliance
Ingram Content Group UK Ltd.
Pitfield, Milton Keynes, MK11 3LW, UK
UKHW021402190726
13845UKWH00028B/821